PRAISE FOR

The Ghost of Christmas Present

"Like the beloved classic *Miracle on 34th Street,* Scott and Amy's timeless Christmas tale works its way into our hearts and charmingly inspires us to see beyond ourselves and embrace the true spirit of Christmas all year long. *'Into the breach, dear friends.'*"

—Maura Dunbar, EVP/Chief Content Officer,
Odyssey Networks

"I simply could not stop reading *The Ghost of Christmas Present.* . . . Books like this serve to remind us of the blessings that we so often take for granted."

—Kevin Carter, college football analyst, ESPN;
fourteen-year NFL veteran; founder of
The Kevin Carter Foundation that serves children
and their families like Braden and his father, Patrick

THE
Ghost of
CHRISTMAS
PRESENT

A NOVEL

SCOTT ABBOTT *and*

AMY MAUDE SWINTON

HOWARD BOOKS
A DIVISION OF SIMON & SCHUSTER, INC.

New York Nashville London Toronto Sydney New Delhi

Howard Books
A Division of Simon & Schuster, Inc.
1230 Avenue of the Americas
New York, NY 10020

First Howard Books hardcover edition October 2012

HOWARD and colophon are trademarks of Simon & Schuster, Inc.

For information about special discounts for bulk purchases, please contact Simon & Schuster Special Sales at 1-866-506-1949 or business@simonandschuster.com.

The Simon & Schuster Speakers Bureau can bring authors to your live event. For more information or to book an event, contact the Simon & Schuster Speakers Bureau at 1-866-248-3049 or visit our website at www.simonspeakers.com.

Designed by Jaime Putorti

Manufactured in the United States of America

10 9 8 7 6 5 4 3 2 1

Library of Congress Cataloging-in-Publication Data

Abbott, Scott, 1962–
    The ghost of Christmas present : a novel / Scott Abbott and Amy Maude Swinton.
        p. cm.
    1. Christmas stories. gsafd I. Swinton, Amy Maude, 1962–II. Title.
    PS3601.B3925G48 2012
    813'.6—dc23
            2012005646

ISBN 978-1-4516-7439-2
ISBN 978-1-4516-6042-5 (ebook)

In memory of
Raymond L. Harris

"To thine own self be true."
—William Shakespeare's *Hamlet*

THE
Ghost of
CHRISTMAS
PRESENT

Chapter 4

THE FOURTH WEDNESDAY

It was the fourth Wednesday of November, and Patrick Guthrie was giving thanks.

Tomorrow there would be no turkey, no cranberry sauce on the side, no dry stuffing to somehow strategically hide under a drumstick so as to not offend the chef. Tonight there was only a slice of pumpkin pie sitting on his son's hospital tray along with a single can of ginger ale, the pop that Patrick and his ten-year-old son, Braden, shared.

"But it's not 'pop,' Pop," Braden said as he grinned. "It's a 'soda.' You've lived in Manhattan for, like, thirteen years. You've got to start picking up the city lingo or you're gonna get your keister kicked out there on the mean streets."

Patrick smiled at the boy lying in the bed, his head balanced on a neck that seemed too thin to hold up such tough words.

"Keister?" said Patrick. "Where'd you learn to talk trash like that? We need to clean up your vocabulary." Patrick lifted the book in his hand. *"Macbeth."*

"Sure," said the boy. "Clean up my vocabulary with the story about the guy who kills his king, then kills his best friend, has the nutso wife who can't stop washing her hands, and then ends up getting killed himself when he thinks that a bunch of trees are, like, walking up to his castle to get him. That's a good clean one, Dad. Yeah, let's read that one again."

Braden had his mother's love of ribbing Patrick about his obsession with Shakespeare, and the father embraced it as the teasing that is allowed inside the intimacy of real love. Especially since it was something Braden had inherited from Linda, Patrick didn't want to discourage it.

But Braden hadn't inherited only the gift of Linda's sly irreverence; he'd also inherited her heart. Her big, generous, and genetically flawed heart. Patrick's wife had been born with hypertrophic cardiomyopathy, an extreme enlargement of the heart that one day suddenly stopped hers, and broke his. It had been just under three years since he'd lost her, since the night she'd gotten up from her barely touched meal only to collapse in his arms at their favorite bistro.

Patrick had buried her, and then, on the advice of the hospital cardiologist, had Braden examined only to discover that the child had indeed inherited his mother's condition. The doctors' consolations and explanations spun around Patrick's brain like debris caught up in the whirlwind storm that was still circling his broken home. The heart condition was "asymptomatic," not detectable through regular physical exams, giving signs of heart abnormalities in only three percent of people before cardiac arrest. All Patrick could think was that it was a cruel irony since he had often said to Linda, "Braden's got your gift for compassion. He's got your heart."

It was the bitter truth. Braden had been born with HCM, as it was called when doctors would sit across from Patrick in offices, or nurses would crouch down beside him as he sat on a chair in a hallway, or a technician would pop his head out from behind a machine's control panel . . . "HCM." The abbreviation made it easier to say. There was so much information to absorb.

A hospital therapist had told Patrick he should bring someone along to the meetings with the doctors, someone who could listen with a calm head and later review all the medical information that was discussed, a family member.

But the sole relation Linda had left did not speak to Patrick, and everyone in Patrick's family was gone. His father had succumbed to cancer not long after Patrick left home, and his mother had died soon after that from a blood clot. Patrick liked romanticizing his mother as the other half of a couple who'd married for life, unable to live on after the death of her soul mate.

But he knew it was nonsense. Patrick's own soul mate had died and he was still here. No blood clot, no lightning bolt, no grand piano dropping on his head. He lived on after Linda's death, if for no other reason than for Braden. Of course he had lived on. Where there was Braden, there was life: his own and, more important, his son's.

So Patrick relied on all the abbreviations to get him

through the days at the hospital, where he walked alongside Braden's gurney as it was pushed down a hallway to yet another test. Then there came the day when the tests stopped, and so did the abbreviations. There was no short way of saying the word "palliative," the kind of gentle care given to terminally ill patients who are simply waiting to die. And that's what Patrick and Braden were told was all they could do: wait.

But that was before Patrick got the call. It came the day he was teaching his students at Independence High School in West Greenwich Village. Patrick, a drama teacher, had just begun his class filled with seventeen-year-olds. He'd grown quite fond of them in his first three months at the school, and to his surprise, they'd taken a shine to him and his flair for acting out Shakespeare and filling the air of the room with his spirit, rather than leaving the old bard to collect dust on the shelves of their young minds.

"All the world's a stage, and all the men and women merely players."

More than a few of the young men in the class were actually listening to Patrick, and more than many of the young women were quite in love with him.

"They have their exits and their entrances and one man in his time plays many parts."

Patrick relinquished his acting pose and sat down behind his desk with his worn copy of *As You Like It.*

"What is Shakespeare saying to us in this passage about life?"

"That everyone's a big fat faker," one boy said.

"Give that man a pair of tights, because he's wrong."

The class chuckled.

"Old Bill is telling us that to find our way through life's drama, we must play a different role in each of its stages. He boiled it down to seven: infancy, childhood, the lover, the soldier, the sage, old age, and then of course decline to death."

The last handful of words brought Patrick's lecture to a silence that settled through the seated rows filled with the young faces who'd heard about their teacher's dying son. A girl in the front row spoke up to fill the quiet.

"Where are we?"

Patrick came to and clapped his hands together, perhaps in some wish to break the spell of his thoughts. "You are all still in childhood, though I imagine many of you are anxious to audition for the role of the lover before you're prepared for that particular part."

A few chuckles and snickers rose.

"You will all, I hope, become soldiers of one sort or another, whether you wear a uniform of public service or simply wear the courage of some cause in your heart. If you do decide to fight for some just cause, you cannot escape the stage of being a wise sage, and it will be your duty to help guide those who come after you. Old age, and then a peaceful decline into death . . . are two stages I wish for every one of you."

Patrick scanned the faces of the classroom brimming with bright futures. "I pray each one of you comes to know all of life's seven stages." But then he leaned forward with a wink. "But to all you would-be Romeo and Juliets out there, take it slow and get to know the family first lest you end up with some really bad in-law issues. And as for film versions, I'm partial to the Leo DiCaprio and Claire Danes film myself."

The students let out a full laugh that pleased Patrick. Everything else in his world had gone into the toilet, but he still had this. Abruptly, the students all stopped laughing as an assistant from the principal's office entered the classroom with a face awash in worry.

"The hospital called. They said they've been trying to reach you on your cell."

Patrick fished out his phone, battery dead again. He looked at the woman and gathered the courage to ask the question that filled every one of his students' eyes. "Is Braden all right?"

"They just said come as soon as you can."

Patrick sat in the cardiologist's office at St. Genevieve's and stared out the window with a statue's stony eyes, blinking only once in a while at the taxis shooting by below on Sixth Avenue. The doctor's chair across from him sat empty.

Patrick had immediately called the hospital, and reached a nurse who assured him that Braden was resting. But the cardiologist had requested to see Patrick right away, and so here he was.

"Mr. Guthrie?"

Patrick rose from his chair and turned to see Dr. Friedman entering her office. "They said you wanted to see me."

Friedman said nothing, only dropped a bound folder on the desk and took her chair.

"They said Braden was resting. Has something happened? Is he all right? I mean—"

"Braden is stable and comfortable. I'm sorry if you were concerned. The nursing staff here is not permitted to pass along the information I'm going to discuss with you."

"How bad is it?" Patrick said as he slumped back down in the chair.

"In this case, Mr. Guthrie," Friedman replied as she took off her glasses, "it's good." She opened the folder. "In the past three months, Johns Hopkins has had great success treating several children with your son's very condition."

Patrick's eyes widened as Friedman's words washed over him.

"I'll warn you up front. It's an invasive procedure, a long time for a little boy to be on the operating table. There are many preparatory tests to be completed and there are serious risks involved, but . . ."

Patrick couldn't help but wrap his arms around himself.

"Your son is a perfect candidate for this procedure. Would you like to hear more?" Friedman paused and looked at Patrick, who could only nod as if in a dream, a beautiful waking dream.

"Go on," Patrick half whispered, not even sure he had said the words out loud, as if he were hovering just under the ceiling watching the scene from a bird's-eye view of unexpected winged hope.

"The operation involves entering the heart through . . ."

But Friedman's medical terms melted one into another and became music, Patrick now hearing only their melody of hope.

And so now, on this fourth Wednesday of November, Patrick sat with Braden sharing the ginger ale and watching his son eat the pumpkin pie, the only food and drink he would be allowed before the angiogram that was scheduled for late Thanksgiving afternoon. There was no question of waiting until after the holiday. If Braden was to have his operation by Christmas and come home with Patrick in the New Year, every day was a chance to take a step closer to that dream.

Earlier, when Patrick had gently explained to Braden that he would be allowed no holiday meal until the operation was over for fear of his vomiting on the operating table, the boy only looked up into his father's eyes and said, quite seriously, "Into the breach, dear friends."

It was from *Henry V*, the Battle of Agincourt scene. If the boy hadn't been so frail, Patrick would have picked him up, carried him onto the hospital rooftop, and shouted to the entire world's horizon, "This is my son! This is Braden Guthrie! He is the bravest soul you could ever hope to know!

"This is my son!"

Chapter 2

❄

COLD FOREVER

The operating room was cold.

For some reason, Patrick thought it would be warm like the hospital nursery he had rolled Braden into when he was born. Why was it so cold in here?

Patrick rubbed Braden's hands through his rubber gloves as the technicians prepared his little body for the invasive procedure. What they were going to do to his little boy had been explained and reexplained to him as if he were being read his Miranda rights. A large needle would be inserted into Braden's inner thigh. This needle would admit a colored solution that would travel through the boy's circulatory system, eventually arriving at his enlarged heart, and there on a video screen, Patrick would be able to see the pumping organ.

"Can we turn up the heat?" Patrick asked through his surgical mask.

The technicians all traded looks from blinking eyes above surgical masks.

"Germs can't thrive in lower temperatures, Mister Guthrie."

"I see."

Patrick rubbed Braden's hands again.

"I'm okay, Dad. I'm not that cold."

But the goose pimples up and down his thin arms and legs told a different story and a small shiver every couple of minutes was its conclusive premise. Patrick pushed Braden's shivering out of his mind the best he could. After all, the boy had endured far greater pain just getting his chin stitched up. That was the time he'd taken his first dive off the diving board at the rec center pool, but then decided in midair to head back to the side. His chin split open and bled profusely into the pool water. Patrick had held him close as they rode in the cab to the hospital, Braden sobbing with pain and the horror of the sight of his own blood.

So this low temperature was nothing compared to that.

Still, Patrick couldn't get out of his head the risks the doctors had warned him about: Braden might go into shock; they might have to do open-heart surgery then and there. And if that were to happen, if the unthinkable were to happen and his boy were to die in that operating room that felt like an icebox . . .

Would Braden be cold forever?

"Are we all ready to go, champ?" Dr. Friedman asked as she entered the room, wearing her mask, gown, and gloves.

"Into the breach," Braden said.

Friedman looked at Patrick, who shrugged. "It's Shakespeare."

"I see. We have an educated young man with us today."

Friedman looked at Braden's EKG, swabbed his inner thigh with a solution that looked to Patrick's eyes like iodine, and then lifted a small needle.

It was much smaller than Patrick had worried it would be, and he and Braden traded relieved smiles.

"Now this is going to hurt a little bit," Friedman said before she inserted the needle into the boy's skin. "That wasn't so bad, was it?"

Braden shook his head.

"That will numb your leg and take some of the sting out of the angio-injection."

And it was then that Friedman lifted a much larger needle, one that Patrick thought shouldn't be put into a horse, let alone a little boy. Braden blinked hard, caught his father's worried glance, and looked away. Patrick held the boy's hand tight.

"Now I won't kid you, champ. This will hurt." Friedman prepared the large needle, filling its casing with a dark solution.

Braden looked back at his father. "Dad?"

Patrick gripped the boy's hand and couldn't bring himself to speak.

"Tell me again about how you met Mom."

Patrick summoned speech like a man pulling every ounce of courage up from his churning stomach to stand it up straight on his tongue. "I met her at Booth One. It was the employees' table at the deep-dish pizza place where we both waited tables."

Friedman finished filling the injection and again swabbed the boy's inner thigh.

"I'd just come back from vacation and stopped by the restaurant to pick up my check."

Friedman rested the needle against the pale, thin skin.

"There she was."

"Beautiful, right?"

"The living reason ancient cities were built and burned."

Braden smiled with the image just before the needle went into his thigh. A tiny tear collected in the corner of his right eye and streamed down his cheek into his ear.

"Then what happened?"

Patrick glanced up at the medical video screen above the table, out of view from Braden but visible to everyone else. There he watched the dark solution enter his son's body and begin its journey through the intricate winding map that was Braden's circulatory system.

"Dad?"

Patrick turned back to Braden, whose left eye had also sent a tear down to his chin and neck. "She said she wasn't feeling well, but since it was only her second day there she didn't want to say anything about going home to the manager."

"So that's when you rode your white horse out of its stable."

"Something like that. I offered to work for her."

"That's not what you said."

Patrick glanced up again to see the dark solution streaming a path closer and closer to the enlarged heart, which beat a quicker rhythm than Patrick had remembered from a minute ago.

"That's not what you said to her."

Patrick looked back at Braden, who was sweating. How could he sweat in such a cold place? "That's not what I said. I said I couldn't let a pair of eyes like hers work when they weren't feeling well."

"Smooth. All that Shakespeare and that's what you cooked up?"

Patrick wanted to wipe the boy's forehead, but he couldn't trust himself to stop there. He wanted to reach down and hold Braden in his arms.

"Hey. At least it was original material. I wasn't pla-giarizing."

Now the solution filled the heart, which beat quicker and quicker. Or maybe it was just Patrick's heart beating faster and faster, like something out of the Edgar Allan Poe story he'd taught his class only four weeks ago at Halloween.

"And she took you up on it?"

Again, Patrick forced himself to look away from the heart, which pumped the solution to all its arteries and four chambers.

"She thought I had a tongue of silver," Patrick said. He fixed his eyes once more on the medical screen, which seemed to grow larger to him, showing the heart beating ever faster, looking ever more vulnerable, as if it would run its last race and collapse right there in front of him.

"Mr. Guthrie?"

Patrick looked at Friedman, whose eyes peered over her mask at him.

"Yes?"

Friedman set her hand on his shoulder and leaned forward to deliver two soft whispers. "Good news."

Braden's arteries were large enough for the actual heart operation.

The whispered "Good news" had danced around Patrick's head like sugarplum fairies drawing overtime pay at the Macy's Thanksgiving Day parade.

When Braden could eat again, the two made a feast

out of the bananas, bland cereal, and pudding he was allowed. Braden pumped Patrick for more and more stories of his mother. Of course, he'd heard them all before, but now he loved listening to them retold by his father, whose voice sounded the happiest it had been in months.

While Patrick sliced the bananas, he recounted the Christmas night when there wasn't a restaurant open in the city except for a stir-fry down in Chinatown, and Patrick had trekked out into the snow when Linda had had a midnight craving for Szechuan tofu. Patrick couldn't find a cab, took the subway for forty blocks, was chased by a drunk, and finally made it home with the white cartons only to find Linda asleep and no longer hungry.

Braden laughed through the pudding at Patrick's tale of himself as a struggling actor dressing up as a talking blender to stand out in front of an appliance store for a Christmas sale.

"I was the best blender that ever worked that sidewalk!"

"No one can be a good blender," Braden said as he fingered the pudding cup for the last vestige of chocolate.

"Of course one can. I created my own character, Sir Christmas Mix."

Patrick jumped up and took center stage in front of the bed. "Yes, ladies and gentlemen. Meet Sir Christmas Mix, savior of the everyday eggnog, liberator of the mundane chocolate mousse—"

"And you weren't arrested?"

"Redeemer of the routine fruit punch."

"Or attacked?"

"I pulled in more business than any blender before me."

"Did Mom know you did this?"

"She helped me rehearse."

"And she still agreed to walk down the street with you?"

"Not while I was in costume. That would have been out of character for Sir Christmas Mix. He was single."

"And Mom still married you?"

"Hey, it paid the light bill, and then some."

"Still, she must have loved you a lot."

At that, Patrick broke out of his performing pose and sat back down on the bed. "Not half as much as she loved you."

"So she'd be twice as happy as you are tonight?"

"Kid, she'd be singing out loud and in public."

And that's just what Patrick found himself doing on Monday morning as he walked down the high school hallway.

"When that I was and a little tiny boy, With hey ho, the wind and the rain."

His voice echoed down the hallway with joyous abandon. He entered the classroom and still sang without embarrassment. "A foolish thing was but a toy, For the rain it raineth every day!"

He dropped his briefcase on his desk. "Sorry I'm late, everyone, but I had a heck of a Thanksgiving." Patrick turned around to his students, to see no one there.

Chapter 3

IT'LL BE A RELIEF

$\mathcal{P}$atrick left St. Genevieve's Hospital and walked west toward the Hudson River through the evening mix of mud and snow. In the two days since he had been laid off from teaching, his life had been a slush of worry and anger.

"Don't you understand I've got a boy facing an operation in three weeks?" Patrick had said to the principal, who could only nod and wipe his head with a handkerchief.

"Your insurance won't pull out on you now. If they do, they'll have a heck of a lawsuit on their hands."

"I'm not worried about my medical insurance; I'm worried about my next paycheck."

"Surely you have some money set aside."

"Whatever money I had saved went to my wife's medical bills. I'm up to my chin in bills just trying to stay afloat while Braden waits for his procedure. And after he gets it, what am I to bring him home to? It'll take my bonus just to keep the lights and heat on, let alone put food in the fridge."

At this last sentence, the principal's face dipped.

"I *am* still getting my Christmas bonus? The checks were to be cut over the Thanksgiving weekend."

"Which is why you were technically let go last Friday. I didn't want to tell you then and spoil your weekend."

Patrick slumped down behind his desk and rested his stunned hand on his nearby bust of Shakespeare. "I'm sorry, but I can't bring myself to thank you."

"I feel terrible about this. You and the new art teacher are the two they chose to let go. Cutbacks on what they consider the 'inessentials.'"

"Where is my class now?"

"They've been incorporated into the Family and Consumer Sciences class."

A school security guard appeared at the door.

"What's this?" Patrick asked.

"He'll see you out. I'm sorry to have to do it, but the art teacher I let go on Friday smashed several ceramic pots on his way out."

Patrick rose in a stupor and went to pick up his Shakespeare bust.

"We'll mail that to you along with your personals."

Patrick was led down the hallway by the security guard as students from passing doorways watched his unceremonious exit. He caught sight of his own kids in the Family and Consumer Sciences class. Patrick broke away from the guard and made a beeline for the classroom door.

"Mr. Guthrie, you can't go in there."

But Patrick opened the door anyway to see the surprised speaking teacher and his saddened students. He struck his usual performing pose with farewell flair. "To thine own selves be true, and it must follow, as the night the day . . . !" But Patrick's voice caved in on itself as he looked at his beloved kids, several girls wiping tears from their eyes.

"Take care of yourselves. Don't forget to live all seven stages."

So now he made his way toward the West Side. Since the passing of Thanksgiving, Christmas had completely captured the city. Decorations and displays burst behind every window. People with packages and bags bustled along the sidewalk, a scene out of the familiar carol, "Silver Bells." "Christmastime in the City," Patrick said aloud as he crossed Tenth Avenue and entered the restaurant where he'd taken up his new job.

Actually it was his old job, at the deep-dish pizza place where he'd met Linda thirteen Christmases and a thousand years ago. Wally the manager was still there. He'd long ago traded in acting for inventory spreadsheets and stock orders.

"Every actor comes to a crossroads when they're twenty-eight," he'd told Patrick some years ago. "That's the magic year when if the magic hasn't happened, it's not going to. If you haven't nailed a supporting role on Broadway or at least five lines in a movie, you're toast." So that was when Patrick got his teaching degree, when he turned twenty-eight, newly married to the love of his life and with a baby on the way.

But here he was back in the employee bathroom tying on a green apron, putting on a white bow tie, and memorizing the specials of the night. He didn't mind waiting tables. It was honest work, and he was always pretty good at chatting up the customers and knowing when to leave them in peace. He was good with people. Wally had welcomed him back with open arms and had given him a host of double shifts Patrick could cover for the other servers, many of whom wanted to head home over the holidays. So the promise of heavy pockets full of tips was blossoming in Patrick's mind and easing him into the idea that he'd be able to waylay the Con Ed ten-day shutoff notice he'd just received for the gas and electricity.

Two things, though, had changed since he'd left. All the servers were new to him; all young fresh faces with young fresh dreams, the very kind he and Linda had nurtured for so long. Also, the customers were gone—at least the steady crowd he'd remembered from before.

What had started out as the promise of quick cash soon turned into the dribble of slow business and bad tips. Deep-dish pizza wasn't New Age Cajun or Thai fusion or whatever people lined up to eat these days—

they certainly weren't lining up here. And when they did pop in for some good old deep-dish, nineties nostalgia, there were more coins than bills left behind as gratuities, and at least once a night the money was sitting at the bottom of a water glass or under an upsidedown salt shaker whose top had been unscrewed. Some cruelties never go out of style. *Season's greetings to you too, folks.*

After his double shift was done, Patrick went to visit Braden, the sympathetic nurses nodding him into where his son was already asleep. Patrick sat next to the boy into the late hours of the night and watched, memorizing every breath the child let in and let out, branding into his brain the rise and fall of the small chest.

When he finally left and arrived home, there was a third notice tacked to the door, a Con Ed final shutoff warning. The next morning, Patrick called every person he and Linda ever considered a friend, even several who hadn't quite merited the word. He'd tossed aside any vestige of pride and went begging, from phone call to phone call. People were wonderful, kind, sympathetic. Some of them remembered Braden as a baby. A few even pretended to remember— Patrick knew they'd never met his son, but no matter.

There were willing to help, but the help came in tens, not hundreds, which wasn't even close to what he needed.

When there was no one else to call, he'd collected just under half of what it would take to pay the rent notice, which had just been delivered by the building's super that afternoon of the first.

"Real glad you're finally getting your bonus, Mr. Guthrie. It'll be a relief to clear up last month's rent and be on top of this one."

"You bet," Patrick said. "It'll be a relief."

Patrick rode the subway in his green-checkered pizza shirt and white bow tie. He'd been too tired after his last double shift to change back into his street clothes. He wasn't fatigued from working too hard, but from standing over a section of tables surrounded by empty chairs. It had been a particularly bad night, and his apron still hung about his waist with less than ten dollars in it.

"Hello, earthlings!" shouted a voice from the other end of the car. Patrick looked up to see a man wearing a wool cap with two antennae sticking up from it that sported two aluminum-foil-covered balls at their tops.

"I hail from the Planet Neptune, and my spaceship has crashed upon your fair orb. I am in need of only a small sum of money to fix my craft and be on my way. If you wish to make a donation to my journey back home, I promise to take Donald Trump with me!"

A scattering of chuckles brought out a few handfuls of coins and dollar bills dropped into the coffee can the alien carried. He walked the car's length, nodding his thanks for each donation. Patrick watched in admiration as the man worked the crowd.

"A five-spot from the lady in blue! For that generous donation I promise to do my best to take Gary Busey too!"

The alien finally stood before Patrick, who could ill afford to give anything away, especially to a man holding a plastic jug in his outstretched hands brimming with bills.

"And you, sir, the gentleman in green. Will you assist a humble space creature in finding his way back home for Christmas?"

Patrick couldn't help but ask. "They have Christmas on Neptune?"

"It's the farthest planet away from the sun, good sir. That's where they need it the most."

Patrick smiled at the thoughtful answer, reached inside his apron, and pulled out a dollar bill. "Have a safe journey home."

And that was how it came to be that Patrick arrived home that evening through the cold winds that blew down his block, and the cold winds that blew through his wallet, with a smile on his face. As he headed up the stairwell of his non-elevator building, he couldn't help but replay the alien's performance in his head.

"Hello, earthlings!" Patrick said to himself as he turned the corner down the hallway to his nearby door, where he came face-to-face with a young woman wearing a serious expression and carrying a serious leather satchel over her shoulder.

"Hello," she said with an inscrutable face. "And may I ask what planet you're just now returning from?"

Patrick stood embarrassed and speechless for a second before trying to muster up the semblance of an explanation. "Excuse me. I just saw a very funny beggar on the subway . . . and I didn't realize you were standing there, and . . . can I help you?"

"My name is Rebecca Brody," she said as she pulled out what looked like an official notice of some kind.

"Ms. Brody, if you're from Con Ed, I'm on the verge of paying that bill in two days' time."

Rebecca's face showed the first sign of any kind of true emotion, and it was ripe curiosity. "I'm not from Con Ed. Why would I be from Con Ed?"

"I don't know. I'm guessing you're not from the phone company or building management, either."

"No, Mr. Guthrie," Rebecca said. "You are Patrick Guthrie, the father of Braden?"

Patrick could only nod as Rebecca fixed her eyes on his face, which was paling with an inner dread rising up through his frame. She put the notice in his hands. "I am from Children's Protective Services."

Chapter 4

A SACRED REALITY

"Are these all you?" Rebecca asked as she studied the wall of Patrick's apartment covered with photographs of himself in different roles, not only in Shakespearean plays, but musical theater and Off-Broadway shoe-string productions; there was even a photograph of a TV screen where he played the role of a Mafia courier in a reenactment scenario for a network gossip show.

"They're all me. The roles of a lifetime," Patrick said, and waited for her to get to the reason for her being there.

"I would think your role of a lifetime would be that of a father."

It was the warning shot he'd be waiting for, the one that told him he was in for some kind of fight, but who or what could have sent her to his door? "I don't consider that a role. My being a father is a sacred reality."

Rebecca pointed to the lone photograph not on the wall, but sitting on a side table next to the couch, framed in a frieze of gold. "Is this your wife?"

Patrick looked at his beautiful Linda. There she was, smiling at the camera from under a wide-brimmed hat she was pulling down over her forehead in the clownish way she used to get past her discomfort with being photographed. "That's my wife."

"Who's been deceased now for three years?"

"Clearly you're not asking these questions, Ms. Brody, but letting me know you already know all there is to know about me."

Rebecca sat down, opened her briefcase, and then remembered herself. "Do you mind if I sit?"

"Not at all. Now will you tell me what this is all about?"

"I'll get straight to the point."

Patrick sat too, several coins spilling out of his apron and rolling across the floor. Rebecca watched them hit the wall and then spin down to rest in the corner. "As I was about to say, this is about money."

"What about it?"

"You haven't got any."

"I'm sorry. Who are you and what do you want?"

"I told you, I'm Rebecca Brody."

"Who sent you? Why are you here?"

Rebecca laid out several papers before Patrick's eyes, which couldn't focus on the sheets but only the young woman's still inscrutable face.

"Several days ago, you were fired from your teaching position."

"I was laid off."

"Let's agree to say you were let go. Let's also agree that you're two months behind on your rent and you've been served a shutoff notice for heat and electricity, though yesterday you did make a payment in person at the phone company, paying in singles and coins."

"Are you following me?"

"I am not following anyone, Mr. Guthrie."

Patrick angrily bolted up from his seat. "Well, someone is following me. So who is it?" More coins spilled out of his apron and scattered across the floor.

"Your partial payment for your heat bill is lying at your feet."

"Listen, I wait tables. I get paid in small bills and coins. That's no crime!"

Rebecca rose with the volume of his voice. "There is no need to shout at me."

"I'd like you to leave, now."

"Not before I give you this." Rebecca took the notice she'd been holding outside in the hallway and shoved it into Patrick's hand.

"You want to tell me what it is?"

"It's an order to appear before a District Family Court in three weeks' time to determine if you are fit to care for your son."

"That's just before Christmas, and how dare you make such an accusation?"

"I do not make the accusation. The city does."

Patrick's eyes filled with thought as a wave of realization flooded his face. "And I think I know who put the city up to it."

"Over the course of the next several weeks, I will be returning to check up on the status of your finances and . . . your heat and electricity. If I find you sitting here alone in the cold dark, I'll know what to say to the board when I give my report. And when they do meet, you'll need to provide proof of employment—"

"I have a job."

"—and a bank statement showing an account with sufficient funds to care for a child. That's a lot of deep-dish pizzas sold to people who aren't sitting at your tables."

"What don't you know?"

"How you're going to get that kind of money. But you'd better get it. Beg, borrow, or steal." Rebecca headed to the door, but then stopped and turned back. "I'm sorry for being brusque. I know most of all that your son's being prepared to have a very serious heart operation, but I can't allow a fragile boy to be brought into an unstable and unsafe environment."

"No one's going to take away my son."

Rebecca opened the door to leave, but not before Patrick added one more thing. "And you can tell Ted Cake I said so."

A wide-framed man stood at a large plate-glass window overlooking the East River toward the Manhattan skyline. His figure was outlined by the setting sun, and his hand reaching into his pocket for his ringing cell phone cut across the red rays piercing the high-end apartment.

"So you see he's not fit to care for that child."

Somewhere in the middle of that city horizon across the river, Rebecca walked down a Midtown street and held her cell phone to her ear against the cold. "That has yet to be determined."

"What information did you gather at your visit?"

"That is confidential, sir. I'll give my report when the court assembles. Until then, whatever information I gather is private."

Silence on the other end.

"Sir? Mr. Cake?" Rebecca waited.

"The man is not fit."

The line went dead. Rebecca put away her cell and crossed the street through the Christmas traffic.

Back on the other side of the East River, Ted Cake stood against the setting sun as if personally overseeing its descent. Then he looked at a piano whose top was littered with framed photographs of a woman in different stages of the same wistful pose, pulling a wide-brimmed hat down over her forehead, shying away from the camera with her hand, grinning uncomfortably at having her picture taken in the first place.

Chapter 5

DICKENS KNEW IT

Patrick sat at Booth One and pored over the want ads wearing the face of a man in search of a drink in the desert. He was in the same seat where he'd met Linda, but this time sitting across from him was some kid with his whole life ahead of him and enough optimism to be circling every audition ad he could find in an actors' directory.

"Is there any part you don't plan on playing?" Patrick asked with a bemused smile.

"You either dream big or live small, you know what I mean?"

Patrick nodded and smiled. "Good for you. Live that stage to its fullest, soldier."

"Huh?"

"Nothing, just something I used to teach to my students."

The kid looked over at Patrick's newspaper, not a thing circled. "So it looks like you're dreaming on the small side today."

"There's nothing out there: computer operators, software designers, wireless technicians. I'm a drama teacher. The most technical I get is when I plug in a reading lamp."

"What about copywriter?" The kid reached over and circled an ad in Patrick's paper.

"I don't know a thing about patents," Patrick said.

"Man, you really are something from out of an old book. It's writing for advertisements. You're a drama teacher. It's like writing."

"I don't know a thing about the ad game," Patrick said as he peeled the top off Braden's fruit cup and set it back down on the hospital tray.

"Are you kidding me, Pop?" Braden said. "You know everything about advertising."

"And how do you figure that?"

Braden sat up and pointed a finger high in the air. "Ladies and gentlemen. Meet Sir Christmas Mix, savior of the everyday eggnog, liberator of the mundane chocolate mousse, redeemer of the routine fruit punch."

"You remember it word for word."

"How could I forget? I'm looking at the man who pulled in more business than any blender before him, and I'm willing to bet every blender since him, too."

So Patrick found himself sitting quietly in the office of a junior advertising executive, wearing a blue Brooks Brothers jacket Linda had made him buy to go to a wedding years ago and watching the young man across from him peruse his résumé with a look of growing concern.

"You have no experience, as in, none."

"I realize I would be new to advertising."

"College grads start out where you'd be starting, and they'd have a marketing degree."

"I have an accomplished theater background as well as teaching drama to high schoolers."

"That's commendable, and I loved 'Phantom,' but what in the world do stories have to do with advertising?"

"Everything," Patrick said, his voice suddenly rising.

Patrick's quiet demeanor was gone, and now a new man sat in his place who even he himself questioned. Was Sir Christmas Mix coming to life inside him? And if his inner blender was being resurrected, maybe that wasn't such a good thing. But Patrick couldn't stop himself.

"Okay, I'm listening," the young executive said in a challenging tone.

Patrick sat forward and readied to do battle, deciding he hadn't quite left his "soldier stage" behind him, as he sure knew he wasn't ready for the "sage stage." "Christmas is your busiest season, yes?"

"Like April fifteenth for CPAs."

"The Christmas you find in church, the real Christmas, well, that's God's creation."

"Agreed."

"But the Christmas you find everywhere else, who do you think invented that?"

The executive opened his mouth to speak.

"Not the deity of Madison Avenue, I can tell you that."

The executive waited.

"Charles Dickens invented Christmas, at least the Christmas we know. And in the story of Scrooge he created the greatest advertisement that the holiday has ever known."

The executive sat back and watched Patrick stand up.

"Before *A Christmas Carol*, Santa Claus was some skinny little elf who looked more like a troll coming to steal from the tots than someone who would leave goodies behind. But in the character of the Ghost of Christmas Present, the fat, jolly, bearded man, Dickens gave us Santa Claus."

"How—"

"I'll tell you how. Because Madison Avenue stole that character for a Coca-Cola ad in the 1940s and presented the world with the fat, jolly, bearded Saint Nick. It all came from a story, just as every advertisement is a story, a tale of a magic potion to make you popular at the prom, or to make the stains on your clothes disappear. You want to sell something; you sell a story to go along with it. Dickens knew it and so do I."

Patrick stopped and suddenly realized he was standing.

"Mr. Guthrie, you've just broken every rule of how to interview for a job on Madison Avenue." The executive stood up, but then held out his hand. "They're gonna love you in the morning bull sessions."

Patrick stood dumbfounded. "I have the job?"

"You have the job. You'll start first thing in the New Year."

"But can you give me a letter officially stating that I am employed here and what my salary will be?"

"Well, no, I'm afraid I can't. You see, it won't be official until my superior comes back in January. But I give you my personal assurance that the position is yours."

"That's not good enough," Patrick said as his face dipped.

"Why not?"

"No, it's good enough for me. It's just that I could

really use that letter before the holiday. There's no way I could get any kind of proof I'll be working here?"

"I'm sorry. Make it through the holiday, and we'll see you in the New Year."

Chapter 6

THE GHOST OF
CHRISTMAS PRESENT

The rest of that day and the next was a parade of disappointment for Patrick. He'd gotten hold of Rebecca at her Midtown office at Children's Protective Services, but she'd made it clear that the court date would not be postponed.

Could not was more like it, Patrick thought. It was Ted Cake who was behind his being investigated; he knew that. How long had the old man been monitoring him? He must have been thrilled when he'd learned Patrick had lost his job.

Ted Cake had never forgiven Patrick for sending his beloved Linda to heaven. That, at least, was the way the old man had seemed to look at it. Linda's father had never approved of Patrick and the love for acting he'd instilled in Linda, nor the "Bohemian" lifestyle to which he'd introduced her.

When he'd met Linda, she was taking a year off between her undergraduate studies and business school at NYU. But then Patrick had entered the picture to change all that, and the old man had never forgiven him for it.

Ted turned his back on his daughter, becoming colder with every passing shoestring production in which Patrick and Linda performed. He'd sent only an obligatory gift when they were married, instead of attending himself, and when Braden was born he'd sent even less.

But then Linda had suddenly died and Ted was left with no one to blame for her death but the son-in-law who'd changed the course of her life. No matter that her heart condition was coiled up inside her for years, waiting to strike. In the old man's mind it was Patrick who had robbed him of his last years with Linda, and now it was outright war.

Ted was coming for Braden to reclaim Linda, or

perhaps just plain old revenge, or maybe a bit of both. Patrick didn't need to confront him to know that.

Now the court date to determine Braden's future was just three weeks away. Patrick had a pillar of bills, no money, and only the verbal promise of employment in the New Year. He had to make it through December somehow and get together enough funds to pass the board.

But here he sat again, at Booth One in his green-checkered shirt, white bow tie, and no one sitting in his section. And again the kid was circling.

"Do you actually go to these auditions?" Patrick asked.

"Not all of them. Some of them. I went to two, a month ago."

"But you're dreaming big?"

"I'm in the planning stages, but I've got to choose carefully. Like here." The kid pointed to an audition he'd put an X through. "There's a production of *The Merchant of Venice* and the parts pay good money, but you need your union card to even get through the door. Now how do you get your union card if you can't get a gig in the first place? Can you tell me that?"

Patrick didn't answer the question. He took the paper and studied the audition ad. Sure enough, the production was paying, and if he'd answered the kid on how to get his union card, he would have given him a speech about being a young soldier. Because that's how Patrick had gotten his union card, and kept up the dues.

 atrick had splurged and taken a cab. It was an expense he didn't need to incur, but the idea of riding the subway dressed in full wig and makeup as the wild-looking Shylock was going to take more courage than he could muster. He'd rather take his chances in public as a blender than the crazed-with-revenge money lender from Shakespeare's *Merchant.*

It had been Patrick's style from the beginning to go in costume to auditions, and he still had his makeup and wigs from the old days stuffed in a beat-up trunk in the closet. So out they came, and into character Patrick went as he rehearsed all last night and that morning for the open audition. The pay wouldn't fill his bank account to satisfy any judge that he could take care of Braden, but it would be a beginning, and it would show that officious Rebecca that he would go to any lengths to keep his son a part of his daily life.

The taxi pulled up to the theater, where Patrick got out and made a hasty jaunt across the sidewalk amidst a few odd stares at his dark-pocketed eyes and shock of bird's-nest hair. He reached the theater's stage door, grabbed the knob, and turned. It was locked.

Patrick's eyes landed on a handwritten sign taped to the adjacent brick wall: "All Parts Filled. Thanks for coming and Happy Holidays!" He whirled around to hail back the taxi, but the cab was already taken and was riding off down the avenue.

Patrick stood there in his wild getup, now a sitting duck for the sea of stares that came his way. This was what he got for still trying to be a soldier. Maybe this awkward spot was the beginning of the wisdom he'd need to take him into his sage stage.

But all the wisdom in the world wasn't going to

keep him warm as he felt the cold whip up the avenue and attack his thin costume. A dollar pulled from his billfold and a quick run to the coffee shop bought him a cup that he now cradled in his hands for warmth as he made his way to the bus stop.

At the bus stop, a line of riders crowded the two benches. Patrick shivered and drank the hot coffee as people passing by threw bewildered looks at his Kabuki face and frantic hair. He leaned against the outer wall of the bus shelter and slid down to rest on his heels. Minutes passed and taxis flew by only feet from his face. He turned around to face the storefronts and sat hunched over with his face down toward the sidewalk, grasping the warm cup in front of him to warm his hands.

Plop!

Drops of hot coffee splashed up across his cheeks in a scalding spray. He wiped them away with an angry hand, but again . . .

Plop!

Passing strangers were dropping coins into his coffee. Again the hot liquid splashed up onto his lips and nose and into his eyes. Patrick looked up in disgust, but all he could see was a blur of passing legs and shoes. What did they think, he was begging for change?

Plop!

He looked sideways in the glass partition of the bus shelter and caught a glimpse of himself. Crikey! He looked like a beggar with a cup out for alms. Patrick didn't think he could sink any lower.

Another handful of coins dropped again, and then a bill. Patrick pulled the wet paper out of his cup and dried it off. It was a single. He turned the cup over, letting the liquid drain onto the sidewalk, and then caught a handful of coins: five dollars and fifteen cents. It was more than he'd made on that table of four he'd waited on yesterday for an hour.

Patrick placed the now-empty cup on the sidewalk, stood up, and studied the round paper vessel as coin after coin dropped into it.

The moment he arrived home, he called the deep-dish place. He'd come down with a twenty-four-hour thing.

They understood. Patrick sat in his apartment in front of the bathroom mirror, his old acting makeup case out. The small jars of face paint, liquid latex, spirit gum, and patches of facial hair lined the shelf just under the medicine chest. The Shylock mask was gone. He wetted a sponge under the faucet and began to apply an undercoating of pancake in a white skin tone.

Patrick looked at his handiwork of the last half-hour. The face that confronted him looked like something out of a Victorian Christmas lithograph: a white-powdered face, rosy red cheeks, outlined lips, and a bushy beard all topped off with a large curly wig he'd worn years ago in a production of *A Midsummer Night's Dream*. From the small Christmas tree in the far corner of the apartment he picked two small ornaments and hung one from each ear. He put on a green velvet robe he'd once worn in *Julius Caesar,* taken from the back of Linda's closet, where he still kept all her costumes. And last, he took the green wreath from his own front door and set it down around his head.

He stood in front of his living room mirror and looked at himself from head to toe. Two pillows from the couch stuffed under his robe completed the picture. Patrick smiled at himself and let out a large Christmas-cheer laugh, letting the sound echo through the apartment like a child's bouncing red ball.

"I am the Ghost of Christmas Present!"

Chapter 7

STILL THE MAN IN GREEN

The next morning, the Ghost of Christmas Present descended the stairs into the Midtown subway station. One head turning led to two heads turning, and that gave way to a gasp and then a chorus of laughs as people parted in front of him. He swiped his Metro-Card and pushed through the turnstile.

Necks craned the length of the station to catch a look at the large, green-robed, bearded man standing on the platform who stared straight ahead. The arriving train pulled into the station, came to a stop, and its doors opened. The Ghost stepped into a car and walked past faces that looked up at him with laughs and great smiles.

The Ghost didn't say a word but walked to the far end of the car and took sanctuary in the corner. Patrick looked down the length of the subway car, every face staring or whispering, and chided himself for thinking this was a good idea. What was he thinking, that he'd hit the streets as the incarnation of the spirit who'd taken Ebenezer Scrooge through the present-day journey of his Christmas world? Yes, that's precisely what he'd thought was a terrific idea only last night, but now it seemed madness.

The train pulled into a station as people got on and off. He decided he'd jump off there as well, run home, rip off the insane costume and character, and head for the deep-dish pizza place. But his feet stayed put and the doors began to close.

Suddenly they opened again at the last second as a late-arriving passenger jumped on board. "Hello, earthlings!" shouted a voice. Patrick's mouth spread into a smile as he recognized the space traveler, still wearing a wool cap with the two antennae made of aluminum-foil-covered balls. "I hail from the Planet Neptune, and my spaceship has crashed upon your fair orb. I am in need of only a small sum of money to fix my craft and be on my way. If you wish to make a donation to my journey back home, I promise to take Charlie Sheen with me!"

The car broke into laughter as the alien made his way down the line of people. "A one-spot from the man with the red shoes! I thank you, and my wife, two children, and dog back on Neptune thank you."

The alien finished with the long line of people and came out of the crammed crowd to suddenly see Patrick standing there. It was then the alien's smile collapsed. He walked up to Patrick and stuck a dark scowl in his face. "You working my train?"

Patrick shook his head, but the alien wasn't buying it. "You plan on working my train?"

Patrick finally found his voice. "I'm going to find my own place. Don't worry."

"How can I trust you?"

Patrick thought for a second and then leaned into the man's ear. "Because I'm still the man in green."

The alien cocked his head in confusion and looked at Patrick's green robe. "What you talking about?"

"I won't mess with your Christmas. I know Neptune needs it most of all . . . being the planet farthest from the sun."

The alien's eyes widened with recognition. "You? From the other day?"

Patrick nodded.

"Why's someone like you doing this?"

"For the same reason you are, my family . . . though they're here on earth."

The alien nodded and then looked at the empty coffee cup Patrick held in his hand. "That gonna be your bank?"

Patrick nodded.

The alien reached into his can, took out a dollar bill, and dropped it into Patrick's cup. "Merry Christmas," said the alien, and he moved into the next car.

The train stopped at a station where the signs read 34th STREET. The doors opened and Patrick waited for the commuters to disembark before he got off.

He walked to the stairs as the morning light from the street shone and the street sounds of Broadway bounced down into the station in echoing waves. He caught sight of himself in the plastic window of the token booth, where the transit workers shook their heads at his appearance.

Perhaps he had gone too far with the costume. Perhaps he had gone too far thinking he should even attempt this madness. Perhaps what was worst of all was even thinking he could save the semblance of a life that he had carved out for himself with Braden.

Maybe Braden would be better off without him in his daily life. Maybe . . .

Patrick shook off the thought as the noise of Broadway waited for him above. He drew in a breath and exhaled. "Into the breach, dear friends."

He began to climb the stairs.

Chapter 8

SPARE SOME COIN

The young woman's laugh rose above the heads of the lunch-hour crowd. Passersby couldn't help but glance back to where she stood in front of the jolly green giant. It was an odd sight, a costumed creature of the streets addressing a hip young woman in her early twenties accompanied by a stylish man in his sixties.

"Sing it again," the young woman said.

"Here comes Mistletoe that is so gent, to please all men in their intent," sang the bearded and rosy-cheeked man as the girl tapped her toe in time. "But lord and lady of this hall whosoever against Mistletoe call, whosoever do against Mistletoe cry, in a leap shall he hang full high, whosoever against Mistletoe do sing, may he weep and his hands wring."

"So it's an old ditty designed to get girls to give up kisses."

"Pretty racy stuff in medieval times."

"Pretty racy stuff now. You be careful you don't sing that to the wrong woman. You'll end up in jail."

"Or in love," he said.

Mila laughed as Patrick glanced at the silver-haired man looking at his iPhone.

"I believe your father has business to attend to."

"He's my uncle, and he wields way more power over me than either a father or an uncle. He's also my boss, at least for another week."

"But I am right, am I not, sir? You are a busy man?"

"You are, and I am," Ted Cake replied as he looked up from his iPhone to the panhandler's Christmas clown face, to which he still had not grown accustomed. Before last week, Ted never would have dreamed of letting a begging nutball like this say more than three words to him, let alone to his niece, but this bum, if a "bum" was what you'd call him, was different.

This panhandler was nothing like the others he had seen come and go on Broadway through the years, listlessly sitting in front of homemade signs that proclaimed they would work for food. If they were so anxious to seek employment, perhaps a hot shower, a collared shirt, and an hour with the want ads might prove a better recipe for success.

The truth was, years ago Ted had been a soft touch for panhandlers. He regularly reached into his pocket for any who asked. But over time he began to despair at his paltry offerings of relief for what seemed to be a relentless river of never-ending need. No matter how much he gave, there was always another outstretched hand. He felt powerless and guilty and frustrated. Impotent. So Ted began to avert his eyes and shut down until finally he stopped seeing the beggars altogether. Better to feel that they were somehow responsible for their own troubles. Better not to feel much at all.

But again, this one was different.

It was seven days ago that Ted had first heard the sonorous voice as he walked with Mila, negotiating their way through the sidewalk's lunch bustle.

"At Christmas I no more desire a rose than wish a

snow in May's new-fangled mirth. But like of each thing that in season grows!"

Ted had stopped mid-stride and couldn't help but peer over the crowd to discover where the voice was coming from, a voice quoting Shakespeare of all things, not what one would expect echoing out amidst the din of the afternoon crowd. But there he was, this bearded, curly-haired, overgrown green sprite clutching a rose in his hand.

"So you, to study now, it is too late. Climb over the house to unlock the little gate."

The man was a cartoon, his face a mask like something out of a Christmas circus. But his voice was captivating. Ted couldn't help himself and recited the next line aloud. "Well, sit you out: go home, Biron. Adieu."

The line escaped out of Ted's mouth before he knew it, and his niece stared over at him in wonder.

"Uncle Ted?"

Ted looked at Mila with the same surprise in his own eyes. "I used to study Shakespeare, in school, when I was a boy." Ted collected himself and turned to guide her back out of the Broadway crowd, but the beggar was before him in an instant.

"No, my good lord: I have sworn to stay with you."
A wild smile stretched across his lips.

Ted's eyes couldn't help but crinkle at the ridiculous sight in front of him, and he moved with Mila to escape, but the Christmas clown was not daunted.

"A businessman who knows his Bard. That is a rarity in this corner of the world."

Ted looked back at the beggar and nodded. "As rare as a panhandler quoting *Love's Labour's Lost* with a trained tongue."

Patrick bowed with a sweeping flourish, one hand completing the dramatic bow, but the other holding up the cup. "Spare some coin for the Ghost of Christmas Present. It will secure you place in heaven, good sir."

Ted's natural instinct was to turn and walk away. It wasn't his job to save the world. He gripped Mila's arm to go. Then his eyes met those of his niece.

"Why don't you give him some money?" she asked.

"I don't reward panhandlers who approach me."

"But Uncle," Mila gently reminded him, "you spoke to him first."

Indeed.

SCOTT ABBOTT and AMY MAUDE SWINTON

And now, a week later, Ted, who hadn't given any money to a beggar in years, found himself once again fishing into his wallet to reward this singing mendicant. Indirectly, that is. "You give it to him. And I should take it out of your Christmas bonus."

"But you won't. You're not that much of a Scrooge. Thanks muchly, we're obliged to you," Mila said as she took the bill and handed it over. As usual, Ted wasn't completely sure to whom she was expressing gratitude, himself or the green Ghost stowing away the folded sawbuck in his velvet robe.

The Ghost gave a polite nod, and the white-haired man and young woman rejoined the lunch-hour swirl of people who crossed the street toward the white WALK sign.

Mila looked back at the bearded beggar, who waved the rose and then held his cup back up to the business suits passing by. "Merry Christmas. So hallow'd and so gracious is the time!"

Mila turned and followed her uncle onto the far sidewalk and up the stone stairs of an office building where a young woman was just leaving. The woman caught sight of Ted and she made her way over to him. "Your call to my superior worked. The date of

the hearing has been moved up several days. Congrat-
ulations, Mr. Cake."

"Just as I expected. Thank you, Ms. Brody."

But Rebecca didn't offer a "You're welcome" as she
turned and headed down the street.

Chapter 9

A HA' PENNY WILL DO

"Christmas is coming. The goose is getting fat," the voice sang out, its sound sifting through the small crowd that had gathered around.

Rebecca's path was completely blocked as she tried to reach the crosswalk before the sign changed. No luck.

"Please to put a penny in the old man's hat. If you haven't got a penny, a ha' penny will do."

"What is a ha' penny, anyway?" Rebecca mumbled as she turned back to catch a glimpse of the green-robed beggar who stood in the center of the circle of onlookers.

"If you haven't got a ha' penny, then God bless you!"

If a ha' penny was a "half-penny," then why not just call it that? "Jolly Old England," she muttered, and this joker looked as if he belonged there.

Rebecca had recently become aware of this new and colorful panhandler. He had taken this corner as his own, and therefore interrupted the lunch timetable she'd carefully worked out these past seven months spent working in this part of town. Four minutes, door to door, from her office just two blocks up Broadway to her favorite chair at her favorite sandwich café that was just across the street within her view. Twenty-two minutes to order, eat, and pay. Another four minutes back to her office, which added up to precisely one half-hour.

No matter that she was given a whole hour for lunch. Rebecca always took half and never noted it on her time sheet or even made mention of it to a colleague. She knew her supervisors would pick up on the loyalty if they hadn't already. "Make yourself indispensable" was one of her mottos, a catchphrase she'd learned at the business seminar she'd taken to start her new career.

There were more like that: "Give them more than they expect." "Take care of the minutes and the hours will take care of themselves." Rebecca chose one quote each day to memorize, repeating it to herself until it became a part of her. "Make your mistakes your friends" was today's, and she said it again while waiting for the WALK sign to finally change.

But there was one mistake she'd made that she'd had a hard time ever considering a friend. Maybe today would be the day that would change all that. The WALK sign lit up and Rebecca headed toward the café. Maybe today she really would get good news.

"I'm so sorry. I'm just so, so sorry" were the words that kept echoing through Rebecca's brain. And she knew that Julie truly was. They had served together as medical residents. No one knew her better, or how much she would give anything to relive that one decision.

"My father did everything he could," Julie continued. "The medical review board just won't budge on something like this. I thought this time they might see it differently—"

"I'm sure of that," interrupted Rebecca as she reached across the table and briefly squeezed Julie's hand. Then she looked down at her half-chicken-salad-sandwich special. She couldn't bring herself to eat even one bite. Rebecca motioned to the waiter for the check.

"You're leaving already?"

"I'm not really hungry."

"Hey, Rebecca. It was a mistake and now it's over. You've moved on, you have a good job. I just wish I could stop you from being so hard on yourself."

"Thanks, Julie, but I guess I'm still mourning all I lost. Or threw away. Or something."

Rebecca looked at her watch—still twenty-three minutes left in her lunch hour. "And anyway, I'm late."

Rebecca transferred the to-go container to her free hand as she crossed the street with more energy and purpose than she felt. Then she stopped, unsure where to go, knowing only that she had to keep moving and not let her thoughts take hold. The corner that had earlier stood choked with onlookers now lay open before her, with barely a dozen people gathered around the man who turned and looked her full in the face. The new, green-robed panhandler with the ridiculous wreath around his head.

Rebecca, like many others, had guffawed with her first close look at him, but then his voice, the resonant vowels, softened her initial mirth. She watched him with a mixture of merriment and serious fascination.

"But the angel said to them, 'Do not be afraid. I bring you good news of great joy that will be for all the people. Today in the town of David a Savior has been born unto you; he is Christ the Lord.'"

"Luke, chapter two, verse eight," called out a man in the crowd, and the green-robed man turned and fixed a winking eye upon him.

"An educated man, a righteous and religious man," said the velvet beggar as he bowed, waved one hand in the air with a flourish, and held out his other with the cup.

The onlooker grinned. "Nah. Just one who's also watched 'Charlie Brown Christmas' since he was a kid," the man said as he pulled a five-dollar note from his pocket and pushed it into the coffee cup.

"A man of fine sensibilities nevertheless! The Ghost of Christmas Present thanks ye!" cried the beggar as the onlooker and the rest of the crowd moved on.

Rebecca remained silent, staring, wrapped sandwich by her side.

The panhandler moved toward her with a slow step and looked into her face, which was flooded with regret. "Things without all remedy should be without regard."

"What?" Rebecca said when she realized he was speaking to her.

Then, more gently: "Consider it not so deeply . . . What's done is done."

Rebecca allowed the words to seep into her heart. "What's done is done," she repeated as the man standing before her nodded and then smiled.

"*Macbeth*. Act three, scene two. The Bard has balm for every ache of the mind and heart."

Rebecca glanced around to see that the sidewalk now was empty and that she was alone with him. She felt on the spot and searched her handbag for something to give. But Rebecca had only credit cards. She never carried cash, ever. "I don't have anything."

"Then God bless you!" the Ghost softly sang to the melody of his earlier old English refrain.

Rebecca relaxed and smiled, and impulsively handed the man her to-go container.

"I don't have a ha' penny. But how about a ha' sandwich?"

※

Chapter 10

A COMMANDING POSITION

atrick hurried down the alley behind the office building, clutching a plastic grocery bag stuffed with to-go containers. The velvet robe he wore had become a smothering blanket on this unseasonably warm day for mid-December, and the makeup and false whiskers chafed his cheeks. But what truly tore at his mind was Rebecca.

Had she recognized him?

Of course she hadn't. It was impossible. She would have betrayed her recognition of him in some way. She was a social worker, but nobody had that good a poker face. And that was the thing about her,

her face. It was filled with some kind of remorse or guilt, or both, so much so that it was he who almost didn't recognize her at first. She was so human. Almost pretty.

Patrick had almost thrown a *King Lear* quote at her: "I am a man more sinned against than sinning," his anger at having Braden's and his life together perhaps torn apart come the New Year, but her face had stopped him. It was that face she wore, like the inescapable mask of some inner sorrow. An old-fashioned word, *sorrow*, but that was what it was.

Heck, he shouldn't have approached her at all. It was enough that he had decided to stake out the corner just outside Ted Cake's office. Patrick had decided not to confront his former father-in-law—or okay, maybe he didn't have the courage—but he was going to give himself the satisfaction of collecting the money he needed from not only the people who worked around Ted, but now the man himself.

But his encounter with Rebecca was unnecessary and foolish. Patrick vowed he would never make that slip-up again as he turned around an office building corner and headed down a darker back service alley. He had only a half-hour before he had to take up his shift at the deep-dish pizza place. Between begging in the afternoon and the night shifts that Wally kept him on, Patrick had begun to collect a respectable amount of money. It wasn't going to win the day just yet, but perhaps in the end it would win him a Christmas with Braden, and all the weeks and months to come.

But right now he had to make his daily late-afternoon delivery. "Who wants a mint-condition— not a single nibble taken—half a chicken-salad sandwich? It's got—" Patrick opened the plastic container and peered inside—"grapes and nuts."

"Why are people always shoving fruit into meat recipes?" groaned a great bear of a red-bearded man who sat leaning against a Dumpster, wearing a Yankees wool cap and fraying warm-up jacket.

"It's called 'Sweet and Savory,'" another squatter shot back at him.

"It's called 'shoving fruit where it's got no business being,'" barked Red-Beard. "You know I've got a theory."

"Another one?" a couple of voices from the shadows called out in near unison.

"Fruit's got no business being cooked, fried, or especially baked," Red-Beard announced as he started holding court. Patrick looked at his watch, hidden under the robe covering his wrist.

"Consider the fruitcake. My theory is that there's only one fruitcake in the whole entire world. People give 'em to each other on Christmas, but nobody ever eats 'em. You ever actually seen somebody eat a fruitcake?"

The circle of squatters demurred.

"My point precisely. They just pass 'em on to somebody else the next Christmas. So, my theory is that there's only one. It just keeps traveling around the world, going from house to house each Christmas."

"Like Santa Claus," someone offered.

Patrick again looked at his watch—only twenty-five minutes left now to remove his glued whiskers and wig, scrub off his makeup, get back into his street clothes, and get to work. He'd been begging for five days now, and he'd been late two of those days. Wally had offered a friendly warning, and Patrick couldn't afford to lose any source of income right now.

"Except this fruitcake is the Christmas visitor nobody wants. It should be stuck in a yuletide museum, along with the one plaid tie that keeps traveling the globe."

"Guys, I've got to go," Patrick announced as he pulled out another to-go container. "How about a nice carton of almost-warm pasta?"

"Sounds good," said Red-Beard. "But what's the sauce?"

Patrick hung his head. He stood in the back alley, stuck trying to give away the food that had been left at his feet for the past eight hours, completely unaware that he was being closely observed from above.

The gaze belonged to the keenest of observers, whose scrutiny over the scene four stories below was unmatched anywhere in the offices, boardrooms, and executive bathroom mirrors of the whole of Manhattan's midtown.

Mila stood in the window of Ted's office building and looked down to where the Ghost of Christmas Present finished handing out the to-go containers to the men in the alley.

Ted sat at a desk at the far corner of an open

office floor where long rows of empty cubicles sat lined with bare shelves. He looked over a private investigator's report on Patrick's state of affairs, or lack thereof. A great stack of chairs stood in the corner, covered in plastic, waiting to be unwrapped and peopled with employees who had yet to be hired to fill the growing ranks of his medical supply company. It had grown from a blossoming corporation into a conglomerate that had its hooks in every hospital in the tri-state area, and gave him more than enough heft with social services to ensure Rebecca Brody's supervisor made sure she did his bidding.

Mila studied the Ghost as he made his way back up the alley and away from the men who devoured their food. "Uncle Ted."

"Hmm."

Mila turned away from the window and regarded the newly renovated office space. "You were right to put your office at this end: it gives you a 'command' position. According to feng shui."

Ted nodded absently. "Hmmm."

"Once I've left to go live in London, who are you going to get to pester you?"

Ted set down the report and offered a rare smile. "I'll see to that."

"My cousin's son, Braden?"

"Just focus on your studies and let me worry about it."

"Why is it that I never met Linda, or her boy?"

"Long time ago; doesn't matter now."

Mila drew in a breath of courage. "If you don't mind my saying, a boy should be with his father on Christmas."

"As my niece, I give you a lot of leeway. Don't press me."

"You can't fire me. I'm leaving anyway."

"Ah, but I can withdraw the offer I'm about to make to pay your tuition abroad."

Mila stared, then laughed, "Ha! You had me there for a moment, Uncle Ted. Great poker face."

Ted smiled. "I'm serious. Studying full time at the London School of Economics is a full-time job. I want to cover your tuition, Mila, so that you won't have to wait tables as well. It's a gift."

"I'm speechless. I mean, thanks, but it's too much. I mean to say—"

"Don't say anything. You're the smartest and hardest-working combination niece and assistant I've ever had; you've earned it. And believe me, I intend to benefit fully from your advanced education once you come back to work for me, so you see my motives are completely selfish." Ted chuckled, then paused. "Please let me do this for you."

"Thank you. You're the most generous man I know."

Embarrassed, Ted returned to the file as Mila regarded him for a few moments. *People never fail to surprise you*, she mused. Thoughtfully she returned her eyes to the window where, below, the Ghost made his way back around the building toward Herald Square. Mila tracked his movements as she walked past window after window, eyes never leaving the robed panhandler.

"You remember the Ghost of Christmas Present?"

"You mean the panhandler?"

"He's got a child he's taking care of."

Ted dropped his pen in affectionate exasperation and sighed. "That man has no family to speak of." He returned to the file. "Next time, just take a look at him. He's a lunatic making a mockery of himself for money. If he had family, they would certainly intervene. Besides, if he had a child, he would make use of that in his performances to foster pity. No, the man is alone in this world."

Mila looked back at the beggar, who moved through the late-afternoon midtown crowd and headed for the subway. "But he does speak about his child. He talks about it every day on the street. You just can't hear it because the kid's cradled under all his songs."

"You're not making any sense. How could you possibly tell that panhandler has a child?"

Mila kept her eyes fixed on the beggar as he crossed the street and approached the entrance to the IRT. "He was wearing a Captain Pluton Band-Aid on his finger."

"A Captain Pluton Band-Aid? Really. If you're creating this annoying fiction as some kind of fond farewell, it's not working."

"He's wearing a kid's Band-Aid."

"Then he got it at a shelter, or the nuthouse for wayward beggars who dress up as storybook characters."

"Those Band-Aids just came out yesterday, same day as the movie. A homeless place wouldn't have them. They'd have the regular kind. But a child might have them, if their mother or father bought them special."

"Mila, the man's a con artist, pure and simple, end of story."

Mila watched the beggar head into the subway and disappear. She said softly, "No, he's not."

Chapter 11

❄

THE AUTHENTIC ELF

Patrick entered Grand Central Station and rushed through the commuter crowd that streamed toward so many homeward-bound trains. Several days ago he'd picked out a bathroom in a distant corner of the great terminal to disrobe and wash off his disguise in private. It was the only reasonably private place he could find between his begging corner and the pizza place.

He'd made the mistake two days ago of sneaking into the back alley of the restaurant still wearing his beggar disguise and there had come face-to-face with Wally smoking a cigarette.

"Auditioning for a role in a pro wrestling staging of *The Nutcracker*?" asked the cynical ex-actor.

"No, I heard Macy's was trying to flesh out its Santa scene this year."

"So you decided to show up looking like Henry the Eighth in his fairyland period?"

Patrick wouldn't make that mistake again, so he'd cased out every possible place between Broadway and the pizza place down on the lower West Side. No subway public bathroom was even close to being safe. A knife at his throat would mean his money gone, or worse. Any restaurant or café was obviously out of the question. Drugstore or supermarket restrooms were too risky; someone who saw him enter would call the cops. Patrick didn't need that kind of hassle.

So Grand Central it was, and this bathroom was perfect. This wing of the terminal was under reconstruction, hence no passengers with prying eyes or panicked reactions. A row of empty urinals and stalls stretched out before him on either side.

Patrick stood before the restroom mirror and heaved the coins and bills from his robe pockets onto the sink's counter. It was a relief to have the weight off his frame. At the week's beginning he had gone to great lengths to bow with a low flourish, but a thousand nickels, dimes, and quarters had tutored his spine to act the part with no problem.

Patrick looked at his watch: nineteen minutes left. He'd practiced this routine several dozen times at home, peeling off the beard and spirit gum, washing off the pancake makeup and rouge, changing into street clothes, and bagging everything into a bundle in just under four minutes. But he'd initially forgotten that he'd have to somehow deal with the day's coins, which again sat before him.

Everything he'd made up until that day had already been carefully packed into hundreds of paper rolls. That's how he'd gotten the darn cut on his finger. The penny rolls were so tight that soon enough their edges sliced, deeper and deeper, into the skin of his pointer digit. But he'd finished the mountain of coin rolls himself. Like heck would he take his earnings to the grocery store where some machine would steal 10 percent to cash them in. The first five days of the three weeks he had to beg were gone, and every penny was precious.

Patrick went to work, peeling off the beard and spirit gum from his chin and sideburns, a large bit of the gum here and there always getting in his hair. If he couldn't easily pull it out, then manicure scissors would have to cut out a chunk of hair. This he'd had to do a number of times, so much so that his hairline had begun to take on the jagged shape of a butchered hedgerow.

Now for the splash of water across his face and the thick coating of Albolene makeup cleanser to scrub off the theater paint. Even as a young actor he'd always hated the post-performance scouring of the oil-based foundation. But off it finally came, and Patrick looked at the mirror to once again see himself . . . and a police officer standing behind him.

Patrick turned around to read the man's badge pinned to his blue chest. He wasn't a street cop, just a transit cop; the shield looked like a tin toy. But the gun hanging from his belt and the baton in his hand were real enough.

"Now what variety of Halloween do we have here?" asked the policeman, who approached Patrick swinging the baton from the strap wrapped around his thumb.

"I'm not dressed up for Halloween."

"Well, seeing as how it's five weeks past, I'm happy

to hear it." The cop was now next to Patrick, looking him full in the face. "What are you dressed up for then, friend?"

"A costume party."

"A costume party? On the first Friday afternoon in December?"

"I was the only one in a costume." Patrick's old improvisational skills had clearly rusted.

"And were other people there to ask you why you were dressed up?"

"There were. They were children. It was a children's party."

"A children's party? And just what kiddie character are you supposed to be?" the police officer asked, looking the green robe up and down. "The Velvet Avenger?"

"I'm . . . an elf." Patrick prayed that God would reach down and take away the shovel he was using to dig himself a tunnel into a prison.

"You're an elf?"

"Not an elf in the way that most people think of elves, little, smiling Christmas creatures."

"Uh-huh?"

"I'm an elf as created by Dickens in his character the Ghost of Christmas Present."

"Uh-huh," repeated the cop, who leaned back on his heels and studied Patrick, who pointed to his costume. "Well, I'd say your Christmas present is looking to have a dim future."

"I'm the original spirit of Christmas. I'm the authentic elf."

The cop looked at the bag of coins sitting behind Patrick on the sink counter. "So all that change wasn't pickpocketed?"

"Those are tips."

The policeman pushed his baton through the loose change and bills. "The parents tipped you all this for a kiddie party?"

Patrick swallowed. " 'The habit of giving only enhances the desire to give.' Walt Whitman."

The policeman nodded and then lifted his baton to rest under Patrick's chin. "The habit of you coming back here again will get this stick shoved in your ear. Transit Officer Sean McKnight."

Patrick had wasted nearly ten minutes conversing with New York's finest and he'd been forced to take a taxi down to the lower West Side and hop out with the driver yelling after him, "Hey, what's with all this silver?" He ran into the front of the restaurant and past Booth One with Wally yelling after him, "Late again, Patrick."

He expected a slow night and that's exactly what he got, but what he didn't expect at his shift's end was to look up to see, sitting in the middle of his section, Rebecca Brody.

"How are you, Mr. Guthrie?"

"Tired, Ms. Brody. It's been a busy night."

"Really," she said as she took a quick survey of the empty place.

"It was busier before. The dinner rush is over, and I've dumped most of the over two hundred dollars I made tonight in my locker in back."

"Two hundred? That's very respectable. Have you been earning that on a consistent basis?"

"Every day. People have really been getting into . . . the Christmas spirit."

"I see. Well, then you won't mind my seeing a bank statement soon."

"Not at all. Give me chance to deposit my money over the weekend and I can have it for you on Monday."

"Very well," Rebecca said. "In the meantime, I'd like to order a deep-dish pizza, whatever kind you recommend."

"Are you sure? You'll feel like you've been hurled back into the 1990s."

"It's a decade I remember fondly."

"Why's that?"

Rebecca paused for a moment.

"I still felt young."

A half-hour later, Patrick cleared her plate and brought her change as Rebecca laid down a ten-dollar tip.

"Thanks for the memories," she said as she rose.

"Hey, I can't take this," Patrick said as he tried to hand her back the bill.

"Of course you can. You provided a service and are now being compensated."

"Why are you helping me?"

"Ted Cake has had the hearing moved up a couple days." She handed him a new court order. "He's got a lot of pull with the city and apparently he's not afraid to pull hard."

"No, why are you helping me?" Patrick asked and

held up the money. "You're supposed to be making sure I can take care of my boy on my own."

Rebecca thought it over for a moment.

"It was something someone said to me today. 'Things without all remedy should be without regard.'"

Patrick ran his hand across his cheek, an unconscious reflex to make sure he really had washed away his makeup.

"I see you working so hard and it's incredible how you're socking away two hundred a day."

"It is . . . incredible."

"So I want to help. Things without remedy should be without regard. But maybe there's a remedy for your case. Well of course you would know that quote."

Patrick's throat closed. "I would?" he croaked.

"You're a drama teacher and it's Shakespeare."

"Yes," said Patrick, becoming more uncomfortable. "*Macbeth.* But I don't remember if it's Act Two or Three."

"It's Act Three, Scene Two," said Rebecca, whose eyes suddenly began to study Patrick's face.

"What is it?" Patrick asked in a nervous voice.

"Who cuts your hair?"

Patrick exhaled and ran his fingers through his slaughtered hairline. "My lawyer said I can't talk about it. It's still in litigation." He offered up a smile.

Rebecca laughed out loud. It was the first time Patrick had seen any kind of joy spring to life in her face.

"Tell your lawyer he has an airtight case," she said, still laughing.

"I was just going for a civil settlement. Should I press criminal charges?"

Rebecca held her hand over her mouth to stop her laughter. When she finally did, she looked at Patrick and said something that only a few days ago would have been the last thing she'd say to this man. "Would you like to go get a cup of coffee?"

And Patrick answered with the first thing that came to his mind. "How about a movie?"

Chapter 12

THEY SHOULD ALL BE
ALLOWED TO HAVE HAIR

"Captain Pluton declares that this Milky Way before us shall stand as our field of combat!"

The animated purple-caped and purple-tongued superhero cut a bold swath across the galaxy, leaving a wake of light behind him that fractured into a rainbow of lavender, plum, and dark grape.

Patrick sat next to Braden in the recreation room of St. Genevieve's children's wing, young folk stretched out before him in the dark, all craning their necks to look at the screen where the new release played. It was a kindness shown by the movie studio to give children too ill to ever have a hope of seeing it in an outside-world cinema the chance to enjoy Captain Pluton and his exploits. A small privilege in an otherwise grim existence.

For these children, it was the world beyond these walls that was a dream. Inside them was the reality of hospital slippers and stuffed baby seals. Baseball caps covering heads in warm rooms, and bathrobe belts too big for waists that grew smaller by the week.

Patrick made a point of keeping his eyes on the movie. He knew that if he looked down at Braden sitting cross-legged next to him, he wouldn't be able to pull his gaze away. And that would only distract the boy and make him self-conscious, but still he couldn't help it as his eyes settled on the profile of all that was important to him.

"Dad, you're staring again. I know I always look too cool for school, but you don't have to point it out to the lady, do you? You're totally cramping my style."

Rebecca, sitting on the other side of the boy, smiled.

"Sorry, buddy."

"It's okay, but if you're gonna be my wingman with women, you've got to let me fly the plane."

"Got it. I'll stick to serving peanuts to the passengers."

Braden looked up at Rebecca, who was clearly amused by the repartee between the son and his father.

"You'll have to excuse him. He hasn't had a date in, like, three years. The only ladies he talks to already have a thing for me."

Rebecca considered the medical reality of Patrick's "love life": all love for Braden.

"Sounds like he's stuck playing second fiddle to a real Romeo."

"I don't have to work hard at it. They all love me for my big heart."

Rebecca reached out and stroked the boy's hair. "I can see why."

Braden leaned over and whispered, "If only Dad would take a night off from staring at me while I'm asleep and put a little romance into his life. It would free me up to nab one of these nurses for myself."

Rebecca looked over at Patrick, whose eyes were fixed on the cartoon where Captain Pluton, in a cape befitting his purple essence, flew across the heavens followed by a host of supporting superheroes.

Captain Pluton's character was the embodiment of Pluto, which had been stripped of its standing as a planet in the solar system by astronomers on earth. So he had a chip on his shoulder and hadn't been willing to help out Angela Earth, even though she was being held captive by her jealous younger sibling, Sister Moon. But now Captain Pluton had had a change of heart and was charging into action. He was now ready to face off with Sister Moon and her minions of comet foot soldiers, who brandished their tails like sabers.

"The fate of the whole cosmos hangs in the balance of the fight we fight here tonight!" Saturnia, Pluton's love interest, proclaimed this as she arrived at the last second and spun her deadly rings into the ranks of the oncoming comet foot soldiers.

You got that right, Patrick thought as he couldn't help but reach out and grip Braden's hand.

Rebecca watched the tight squeeze between the two. Her mind began to churn. She'd worked so hard for so long to bleach herself of any kind of bias. It was her job to ensure the welfare of children; here was a child on the brink of having his heart opened and closed, left to a father who she wasn't satisfied was capable of taking care of him.

Financially, that is. Emotionally, there was no

debate. Patrick was a balm to the boy; that was clear. But Ted Cake had put so much pressure on her supervisor, who in turn dumped it on her: Patrick was months behind on his rent, electricity, heat, the essentials of life, let alone the amenities that could make this boy's complete recovery a certainty.

And Ted Cake could offer those amenities: a huge income and a comfortable place to live. So many material advantages, servants, the best food, vacations for the boy. Her brain went into a full swirl as she reprimanded herself for being in this position in the first place. She'd never wanted to dictate people's lives; she'd wanted to save them.

She'd wanted to be a doctor. Why had she thrown it all away on some ridiculous mistake? It was a mistake that would never be her friend, ever.

Her eyes traveled across the sea of small heads looking up at the screen, knowing she'd been disallowed to treat any of them, now only directed to take one small boy away from his dad and place him with someone who wasn't his parent. Once Ted Cake got his hands on Braden, who knew how long it would be before Patrick could gain full custody again? Maybe only weeks, but then again, maybe months. What if it turned out to be a year? A year in the lifetime of a father and son was just that, a lifetime.

Rebecca felt faint and her breath became strained. She leaned over Braden's head to Patrick. "I'm going to stretch my legs," she mouthed.

ebecca had walked past the same nurses' station three times before she realized she was traveling in a circle, a circle that happened to have four right hallway corners. The children's wing here wasn't as big as at Lenox Hill, but any children's wing at all was big enough.

In her days as a resident, she had decided early on that she would specialize in geriatric medicine. Rebecca had told herself that the elderly were the ones in need of the greatest care. It was they who had married, raised children, contributed to the general welfare of society, and now, in their late stage of life, deserved the best treatment any hospital had to offer.

But now Rebecca wondered. Had she swung the pendulum of her skills to that other side of the age spectrum not out of nobility, but out of cowardice? Was it just easier to care for a human being who'd lived a full life? In her days as a medical student, Rebecca had logged only limited time with sick children. The little ones who'd awakened from birth to a world named after a disease: leukemia, neutropenia, progeria, and on and on. The terms had spun through her mind like a carousel of painted horses carrying no riders.

Was that why she had been drawn to geriatrics? For the same reason she'd told Patrick she needed to stretch her legs, when actually it was her heart that was uncomfortable? Rebecca had seen this gentle man reach out and take hold of his son's small hand. She told herself they needed their privacy.

But what kind of privacy was there in a room packed with little people who lived their lives in a crowd of doctors, nurses, and attendants? Whose illnesses meant endless tests and treatments and procedures that left them completely vulnerable and tore away at any semblance of solitude? Little people who would probably never know what it was like to be bigger than little? Who would never know what it was like to walk down a high school hallway and suspect that they were the biggest geek God ever bestowed on the world? Who would never know what it was like to come down with the flu the very afternoon of their junior prom and then watch from a bedroom window while their date took a visiting pretty cousin instead? Who would never know what it was like to feel the pain that a full life inevitably brings with the very act of living?

These were her memories, not theirs. But would they ever get the chance to have memories? Even painful ones?

Life was full of pain. It was unavoidable, but it was also what gave the joy its own life and limbs. Pain was obligatory. There was no getting around that. But suffering was optional.

Rebecca stopped walking and let the thought stream through her brain and heart. "Pain is obligatory. Suffering is optional," she said out loud to herself.

Here she had been, polishing her guilt and grief over an old mistake whose shelf life had long since expired. She'd given herself a good, self-indulgent dose of suffering. The panhandler was right. "What's done is done."

Rebecca looked ahead down the hallway and saw a child crouched in the corner, busy coloring. She must have passed by the young boy all three times without noticing him. But he was a welcome sight, looking healthy, rosy-cheeked, and clear-eyed. Rebecca approached the boy and looked down to where he was scribbling away with a brown crayon across a hospital pamphlet.

The pamphlet was a brochure for the treatment options for childhood bone cancer. On the cover, a face no more than three years old smiled out from under a hairless scalp.

The boy's crayon drew on hair. He finished the pamphlet, set it down on the pile he had already completed, and moved on to the next.

Rebecca's presence finally caught the boy's attention and he looked up at her, expecting to be reprimanded for defacing the brochures. He met her gaze with quiet defiance. "My sister should be allowed to have hair. They should all be allowed to have hair."

The boy returned to his dogged coloring, his hands determined to restore what had been stolen from his sister, his eyes fixed on fixing his world.

Rebecca studied the child. "Yes," she said to herself, deciding what would be her daily motto for the rest of her life. "Suffering is optional."

Chapter 13

MY SON'S FATHER

"Pain is obligatory. Suffering is optional" was all Rebecca had said to Patrick just before she'd left him at the hospital late last Friday night. That night, her strange farewell played over and over in his mind as he stayed up and stared at his sleeping boy until he fell asleep himself. But when he woke, there was her sentence again, echoing in his mind.

Monday morning, Patrick arrived early in his costume and passed a new Santa for charity, who banged a tambourine and called out for donations. "Make a donation to Coins for Kids. Care for those who can't care for themselves."

Patrick spent the day working his magic on the corner. Rebecca had come and gone, of course not recognizing him at all, but now he looked at her with new eyes. She really had seemed warmer to him when she'd left last night. Or maybe it was just Patrick's imagination, or vain hopes dancing around his head like new sugarplum fairies. Ted and his assistant had stopped by as well. Patrick had even been warmer to him. Perhaps Rebecca's warmth was contagious. But at the end of the day, Patrick stuffed all his bills and coins into his robe and walked past the Coins for Kids Santa, who hadn't done nearly as well. He felt guilty. Patrick fished out a ten and dropped it in the red bucket.

"Thanks!" said the Santa.

"Don't mention it," said Patrick as he continued on.

But still he felt guilty. Ten dollars dropped in the bucket wasn't going to take that away. Was he stealing from people who really needed it? With or without the Coins for Kids Santa, was he stealing? Here he was pretending to be something he was not. But everyone knew the Ghost of Christmas Present was just a role, so perhaps he wasn't stealing but playing a part and providing a service. Or perhaps he was convincing himself of his own lies?

These questions took him around to the back alley where he set down the day's to-go containers. Red-Beard in the Yankees cap and the rest of the squatters huddled in a cold circle around an ash-can fire. "What you serving this evening?" Red-Beard called out.

"Haven't had the chance to look," Patrick replied.

"Potluck? And on a Monday?"

Patrick shook his head and turned back. "Good appetite, gentlemen." He waved his hand and made his way out of the alley.

Waiting at the entrance stood a large, familiar silhouette. Coins for Kids Santa stepped out of the shadows and blocked his way. He sported a great wide smile. Then suddenly the Santa grabbed Patrick and slammed him against a Dumpster.

"Listen to me, you begging sack of crap. That's my intersection! I've worked it for years, and some street freak like you's not gonna steal any of my action."

The Santa held Patrick by his green velvet robe, which began to rip.

"Hey!" The voice came from behind the Santa, who turned to see Red-Beard in his Yankees cap along with the other squatters standing in an imposing semicircle.

"You bums crawl back into your bottles."

Red-Beard stepped up to the Santa and pulled him off Patrick. Patrick straightened his robe as the squatters surrounded the man in red. "We don't like it when Santa Claus gets rough," announced Red-Beard.

"Doesn't feel natural," said another.

Red-Beard reached out and yanked the white beard from the thug's face to reveal a stubble-covered chin. "Well, whaddya know?" Red-Beard said as he looked back to the others. "He's not the real Santa Claus."

"That's a relief."

Red-Beard pulled off the Coins for Kids ID from the crimson coat and tossed it aside. "And I'm willing to bet this wasn't made at the North Pole either. Hit the bricks."

The thug picked up his beard and badge and took off down the alley. Red-Beard looked at Patrick. "All right. We've been meaning to ask. We know you're not the leftover food fairy. Who are you, really?"

"I'm my son's father," Patrick said, and he headed the down the alley the opposite way.

The squatters watched him go.

Chapter 14

❋

A TRUE LABORER

atrick sat by Braden's hospital bed, but he looked out the night window instead of fixing his gaze on the boy as he'd always done. The day had shaken him.

It had started out with such a glow of hope, with recalling Rebecca's observation of pain being obligatory and suffering being optional. It was a strange refrain, but somehow her words offered Patrick the sense that life itself was dropping a whispered promise into his cup that his life as Braden's father wouldn't be interrupted after all.

After Linda's sudden death, being a father had been the most painful thing Patrick had ever experienced. But he had done everything he could think of to keep the suffering outside in the hospital hallway and not in his son's room. He had never broken down into sobs just to hear himself cry. He had never cursed the night clouds just so he could hear his own voice shout, "You've stolen my wife, and now you come for my son?"

Those would have been the outbursts of suffering. And it became clear to him through Rebecca's words that when he had decided to beg in disguise, it was another way he had turned away from any self-manufactured misery and instead embraced the pain that living brings.

But the day that had started out with Rebecca's promising words in his mind had ended with a criminal Kris Kringle. Perhaps Patrick should just go to another corner, find another part of town.

But that was his corner. Those people were his regulars. And he didn't steal their money with a forged badge. He earned it. He was providing a service. A good fifteen or so folks whom he now knew by name came up to him every day with requests.

There was Mindy, who worked in the café across the street. She had a son serving on an aircraft carrier in the Persian Gulf. Patrick had offered up T. S. Eliot for her one day on her way home from work. "At the violet hour, the evening hour that strives homeward, and brings sailors home from the sea."

She'd wiped a tear from her eye, dropped a five in his cup, and every day after that asked him to quote the same line until she didn't need even to ask. It was simply their daily farewell to each other.

Then there was Kent, who worked in public relations. Patrick had overheard him tell a colleague on the street corner that he was planning to ask his girlfriend to marry him at a hockey game that night on the public video monitor. Patrick had not been able to help himself. "O, what men dare do! What men may do! What men daily do! Not know what they do!"

"Excuse me?" Kent was annoyed with the green-robed panhandler who had intruded on their curbside conversation and stood uncomfortably close.

"As all is mortal in nature, so is all nature in love mortal in folly."

The young man's face grew even more confused. "What is that supposed to mean?"

Patrick shook his head with exasperation. "Ask her to marry you in private."

The next week, Kent came up to the beggar with a buoyant gait. "She accepted my proposal! But afterward, when I told her what the original plan had been . . ." Kent handed Patrick a fifty. "Thanks for the safety tip."

And then there was George, the stockbroker with whom he'd had the Charlie Brown exchange. Patrick had taken to memorizing Psalms just for George, who relished the biblical passages spoken with a trained tongue. "Consider and hear me, O Lord my God: Lighten mine eyes, lest I sleep the sleep of death."

"Psalm 13, verse 3." George had never yet been stumped.

"A man well-schooled in both the King James Bible and its benevolence."

George dropped his customary bill into the cup. "Here's a fiver for a man well-schooled in the art of malarkey." George studied Patrick for a long moment. "I can't figure you out. What's your story?"

It was a question that people had begun to ask, and Patrick had wasted no time in looking to the Bard for a comeback: "I am a true laborer. I earn that I eat, get that I wear, owe no man hate, envy no man's happiness . . ."

"All right, all right," George said as he stuffed another bill into the cup. "I'll pay you to put that story
out of its misery. See you tomorrow."

All the questions he'd begun to get about his life
story he'd been able to keep at bay with the *As You
Like It* comeback. But again, there was this thug in
the Santa getup. Would he come back? And would he
come after Patrick again?

If he did, Patrick would just reveal him to the
police as a fraud. Even a couple of the cops who
worked that beat had taken a small shine to the harm-
less robed nut whose only trespass was filling a corner
with clapping laughter.

"Yo! Jolly Green Joker!" the cop riding shotgun
would always yell to him from the open patrol-car
window. Patrick could think of wittier nicknames,
but any officers deciding to leave him alone were as
clever as he needed them to be.

"How's business today?" the cop driving would
add.

"Booming, just like the Jets' chances to make the
playoffs," Patrick would reply.

Patrick knew as much about football as they likely
did about Shakespeare. But he'd decided early on to

lay off the Bard when it came to the cops, and stick to sports. As he had learned in the past, just one misinterpreted line could threaten their easy communication.

"We're going all the way!" the first cop always shouted.

"Super Bowl bound, baby!" said the driver.

"Cry 'Havoc' and let slip the dogs of war!" Patrick had once cried out with hearty exuberance.

"Huh?" said the first cop as his partner pulled the car to a stop.

"I only meant to say . . . We're going all the way, baby!" Patrick answered.

The passenger cop finally nodded. "You said it, Joker."

The patrol car had continued on its way and Patrick vowed to keep to the plain English sports script in the future.

Now he sat in his son's hospital room having decided that he had earned the right to work that corner. Indeed, he was a true laborer. And tomorrow he would be back on the job.

Chapter 15

❋

IF WE SHADOWS HAVE OFFENDED

"I will honor Christmas in my heart, and try to keep it all the year!" Patrick held court on the sidewalk corner in as kingly a manner as he had the entire two weeks he'd claimed that patch of concrete for himself. Four whole days had passed with no sign of the false Santa. Patrick's back-alley boys had scared him off, or maybe it was just that the thug didn't want any trouble and found himself another street on which to thieve.

And now Patrick performed to the largest crowd he'd collected yet. This December Friday evening the commuters were more than in the mood to stop and listen to the beloved beggar recite from *A Christmas Carol*. They were expectant.

"I will live in the past, the present, and all the future."

Mila smiled wide, and even Ted grinned over at his assistant's face and then back to the panhandler, the initial suspicion of the costumed man now transformed into a genuine affection.

"The spirits of all three shall strive within me. I will not shut out the lessons that they teach." Patrick's strong, theatrical voice carried over the dense crowd, past Mindy, who'd stopped even though there hadn't been the chance for their usual exchange; past Kent, who stood with his new fiancée holding a department store bag of Christmas packages; past George, who nodded his head with admiration at the beggar, who was the most tireless spirit that the stockbroker had ever witnessed.

And the voice finally landed in the crowd's far back row, where there stood the thug. Still stubble-faced, but minus the yuletide getup, the thug looked from Patrick over to where his cohort stood on the other side of the crowd. The two men met eyes as the thug put a finger to his nose, but it wasn't because he was about to fly up a chimney.

"Oh, tell me I may sponge away the writing on this stone!" Patrick called out across the circle to Mila, who smiled.

"Put a pineapple ring on your head and call you a Christmas ham!" the young woman yelled, as the crowd laughed and Patrick bowed with his trademark flourishing wave of the hand.

"I am a banquet who seeks not to feed the stomach, but only the ears."

Ted nudged Mila to move on, but not before he reached through the crowd to drop a one-hundred-dollar bill into the beggar's cup. Mila caught Ted's arm as they made their way back to the office, "Did I just see what I think I saw? A Benjamin sailing through the air into a panhandler's jar?"

"Well, he gives good value. And besides, times are hard all over these days. I admire anyone who isn't afraid of looking foolish to take care of his child. Now stop wasting my time—you're on the clock."

Mila smiled to herself and followed.

"What a character," George said as he dropped a large bill into the paper cup now circling its way around the crowd.

"He's our very own Cupid," said the young woman

who held onto Kent's arm as he tucked in another bill and passed the cup.

"I got a letter from my son, who's been given last-minute leave to come home for Christmas," said Mindy happily to no one in particular. "And he predicted it. I don't know. Maybe he even made it happen."

She dropped her own bill into the cup. The crowd didn't disperse, but just stood and watched in wonder as Mindy, the lady from the café who was always short on time and temper, walked up to the green-robed Ghost and embraced him.

Patrick stood still. He was entirely unaccustomed to being touched by the strangers from whom he begged. After all, generosity and compassion for a fellow human only went so far. No one actually touched a street person. In fact, he had come to believe that people gave money precisely in order to avoid personal contact. But then he became Patrick Guthrie again, school drama teacher, father to Braden, and the kind of man who could return a hug to a nice lady who just needed to bridge the gap till her own son was in her arms once more. The crowd broke out in a street-corner ovation.

Mindy stepped back and joined in the spontaneous applause, which slowly died down to silence. Patrick stood alone like an actor on a stage whose rapt audience waited for a final soliloquy. "If we shadows have offended, think but this and all is mended. That you have but slumbered here while these visions did appear, and this weak and idle theme no more yielding but a dream."

The evening crowd listened intently as Patrick offered the weekend farewell. Even the traffic noise seemed to die away as he continued his parting words. "Gentles do not reprehend. If you pardon, we will mend. And as I am an honest Puck—"

"Somebody stole my wallet!" Mindy yelled.

The thug traded nods with his cohort, who moved through the crowd as people began checking their jackets and pants.

"Mine's gone, too!" cried Kent's fiancée.

"And mine!" reverberated through the crowd as the thug's cohort brushed up against Patrick, whose incredulous gaze saw more people finding empty pockets and purses.

"It's the beggar!" shouted the thug.

The cohort grabbed Patrick, who fought to pull away, but the moment he broke free from his grip, a shower of leather dropped from his green robe and rained on the sidewalk. Patrick stood inside the ring of wallets and change purses surrounding his legs and looked up at the eyes that stared back in disbelief.

Patrick picked up what he recognized to be Mindy's wallet and tried to hand it to her. "It wasn't me. I've taken nothing from anyone."

Mindy shook her head and grabbed the wallet away from him. "And my son's service pin was in there."

Helpless, Patrick looked out as the crowd rapidly descended into a mob. "It wasn't me. I p-promise all of you," he stammered. "Someone has done this to me!" he yelled just before he caught the eyes of the thug. "It was him! He's a fake Santa Claus who works this street with a fake charity badge—"

"Call the cops!" cried Kent.

But there was no need. The patrol car was already being waved down by the cohort, who wasted no time in spinning his lie.

Patrick saw the flashing lights go on as the two policemen jumped out onto the street, and he turned and hurried toward the far end of the crowd. But a couple of men stepped up to block his way. "Not a chance, buddy."

Patrick swerved in another direction, but again the crowd cut him off from any avenue of hope. There was only one possible way out of the crowd: in the grip of the two cops, who grabbed him and dragged him to the waiting car. "All right, let's go!" One of the policemen slammed Patrick up against one of the back doors and cuffed his hands hard.

"I get it now, Jolly Green Joker," said the shotgun cop. "You stage your own little Christmas pageant just waiting to pickpocket everyone's candy canes."

"I swear—" was all Patrick could get out before the driver cop shoved him in the backseat.

"Save it for your new cellmates. I know some boys inside our cages who love a good bedtime story." The two cops climbed into the cruiser's front seat, which was separated from the back by thick steel meshing.

Patrick put his hands and face to the wire. "But you don't understand. You have to listen to me."

The driver started the engine as the shotgun cop addressed Patrick. "When you join the NYPD, they tell you that you don't have to listen to bums who pickpocket people at Christmas. It's like a regulation or something."

The patrol car pulled away from the curb. Patrick turned to the back window and watched the crowd disperse. He couldn't find Mindy or Kent or even George. But he did find someone. It was Mila standing there with Ted. Her eyes and Patrick's met as she watched him being driven away.

"I didn't do it," Patrick mouthed, but before he could finish his sentence, Ted had already turned the young woman around to lead her away.

Chapter 16

WANDERERS OF THE DARK

Midnight Manhattan splashed itself across the horizon in a blurry Milky Way of traffic signals and blinking neon. Here and there, wandering cabs trolled the streets for stray merrymakers looking for a dry ride home from their holiday cheer. One taxi driver gave up searching for a new fare and peeled off the East River Parkway to head across the Brooklyn Bridge.

Ted sat in his cashmere dressing gown and watched the lone taxi from his apartment window as it drove over the river and wound its way around an off-ramp before disappearing into the wet backstreets of Brooklyn Heights. "The wrathful skies gallow the very wanderers of the dark and make them keep their caves."

"What did you say, Uncle Ted?"

Ted looked up to see Mila standing behind him, having just let herself into the apartment.

"Nothing," he said and pulled his gown tightly around him. "What are you doing here so late?"

"I came to drop off these papers. I worked overtime to get them done. I've got a lot of packing to do before I leave. Why are you talking to yourself in the dark?"

"I don't answer to my employees. They answer to me."

Mila set down the stack of papers.

"This is the last of my work. I'm no longer an employee."

Mila came over and curled herself up on the far end of the leather couch.

"Poof, I'm once again your niece."

"Who taught you how to talk?" Ted asked with a wry grin.

"The one who was always there for me while Mom

was off memorizing the beaches at Costa Del Sol . . . you."

"My sister's a good person. But it's a fact she often forgets."

Ted reached out and gripped his niece's hand.

"What were you saying when I came in?"

Ted exhaled. "I was reciting a line from a play. *King Lear*."

"I've heard the title. What's it about?"

Ted looked out the window at the dark downpour splashing across the glass. "It's about an old man with a long white beard who talks to himself in the night rain."

"You're behind on your beard."

"I don't think the shareholders would care for an unshaven CEO. I knew a corporate president once whose two-day stubble sparked rumors of a no-confidence vote."

"So why are you reciting a play to yourself in the night rain?"

"Because, like Lear, I'm going crazy. Isn't it obvious?"

"You're going to miss him."

Ted offered her a quizzical glance.

"Please don't pretend to not know who I'm talking about," Mila said.

"I am going to miss him," Ted conceded. "Nothing but a con man, as it turns out."

"We don't know that. Not for sure," Mila said. "But even if he is, there's a child involved. His child, I'm sure of it."

"Because of a Band-Aid. That again? He's a con man simply out for himself," Ted said as his face darkened and he looked at his pictures of his beloved Linda. "All actors are con men."

"Why do you say that?"

"I didn't say that. My father did . . . when I announced that I wanted to be an actor." Ted rose and walked over to the wide glass window.

"You? An actor?"

"Is it so hard to believe?"

"No. Well, maybe a little. It's just that I never knew. Were you any good?"

"Good?" Ted said as he turned and spread his arms out, the wet, smeary lights of Manhattan behind him, the folds of the cashmere dressing gown draping him in the guise of an ageless lord from some lost kingdom. "All the world's a stage and all the men and women merely players. They have their exits and their entrances and one man in his time plays many parts."

Mila's face betrayed what Ted hoped it would. He was good.

"So what parts did you play?" Mila asked.

Ted dropped his arms. "Just one. The role of junior medical administrator. Only to be elevated after several thousand performances to the role of senior medical administrator."

"That's why you approached the beggar last week. You studied the theater. That's how you knew what he was quoting."

Ted sat down and stared straight ahead. "I hadn't seen a Shakespeare production in forty years. But the moment I heard that panhandler's voice, it was like the sound of a dream I'd purposely misplaced somehow finding me anyway."

"What happened to make you misplace your dream?"

"Eustace Cake happened. Our venerable old ancestor, Colonel Eustace Cake, the hero of the Battle of Antietam." Ted walked over to a near wall, where a carefully preserved reproduction of a Civil War daguerreotype hung in the shrine of a solid silver frame. "The inventor of the Mobile Surgical Hospital, founder of the family medical supply company, and all-around inescapable family legend."

"But *he's* been dead over two hundred years."

"That's the funny thing about legends, young lady. You'd think they'd fade over time, but they only grow larger. And there was no chance the great-great-grandson of Eustace was going to tramp off to follow the path of a thespian."

"A 'thespian'?"

"It was not to be an actor's life for me." Ted pulled his robe tighter around himself and retied its knot. "But that beggar. I believed in him," Ted said to Mila as he continued with uncharacteristic candor. "I could see no real purpose for him to be on that corner, no constructive economic upside, no supply and demand that was realized or fulfilled. But I believed in his presence. Now he's gone, just another con man overcrowding another jail. A thing of the past."

Ted headed up the spiral staircase to his bedroom

before calling down to her, "I'm suddenly very tired. I'll call the car service to take you home. Good night, my dear."

Mila shivered and looked out the rainy night window. "Where are you tonight, our Ghost of Christmas Present? And are you now a Ghost of Christmas Past?"

Chapter 17

THE GHOST OF CHRISTMAS PAST

atrick rested closed-eyed on a gray metal cot, his green velvet robe draping over its frame and brushing the cement floor, his head-wreath hung from an iron hook. It was only just past one A.M. according to the NYPD clock on the cell-block wall, and it had already been the longest night of his life.

Visions of being dragged out of the patrol car and thrust before the desk sergeant played out in Patrick's mind in a parade of half-dreams: the passing faces of the precinct guffawing at his costume, the cackles at his makeup, beard, and wig, the laughter as he was hauled down hallway after hallway only to be tossed in lockup.

"If you're gonna bring a clown in here, he'd better be able to juggle!"

Patrick had forgotten what it was like to feel the ridicule that first greeted him when he'd established his corner. In the two weeks since he'd begun begging, not only had he collected enough to pay off the electricity, heat, and one month's rent, he'd also collected a small crowd of hearts whom he'd touched.

He hadn't set out to do so, but it had happened, and its happening had made him think that this whole panhandling endeavor was imbued with some kind of magic. But it hadn't really been magic. It had been theater, living, breathing theater right out there in the streets, just the kind that modern American playwrights had dreamt of staging in dockyards and warehouses and places where people actually worked and lived out the drama of their daily lives.

And he had done it. He had taken his own brand of dramaturgy out of the theater and staged it during the morning commute, then lunch hour, and finally the five o'clock rush hour. Three shows a day, with intermittent repartee and pedestrian requests to fill in the pre-lunch and mid-afternoon lull. He was a medieval troubadour romancing the minutes of an ordinary day for coin.

But now it had come collapsing around his green robe in a ring of stolen wallets. He hadn't even felt them planted on him, it had all happened so fast and with such frenzy. He'd panicked and completely shut down on the police who'd demanded to know who he was.

Patrick had told them nothing—not his name, or why he was there on Broadway, or even that he'd been framed. He hadn't carried a wallet for fear of anyone knowing his real identity. Heaven forbid he should be found out. If it got back to Rebecca and then Ted, it would be over. Braden would not only be taken from him for financial reasons, but the board would make a Christmas feast out of his mental state. Any visitation he might be afforded would be in jeopardy as well.

He would be supervised in Braden's presence, perhaps never again having the boy to himself. So Patrick simply stayed silent at the cops' questions and decided to wait until things had calmed down before figuring out how to proceed. Even the one phone call he was allowed he made to Braden, keeping his voice low, cupping his hands over the mouthpiece for privacy.

"What time you gonna get here, Dad?" Braden's voice was soft but cheerful.

"I'm afraid I'm not going to be able to make it tonight, buddy," Patrick whispered.

"Late shift at the pizza place?"

"Yeah. Late shift. I'll see you tomorrow, okay?" He clenched his eyes shut, willing it to be true.

"Okay, tomorrow. I'll save my dessert cup for you."

"You don't have to do that."

"It's French vanilla, Mom's favorite. We always clink our spoons together and share it."

Patrick opened his eyes and for the first time in as long a time as he could remember, water collected in their two near corners. "Right." Pause. "We'll clink our spoons together." He swallowed.

"You okay, Dad?"

"Let's go, Jolly Green!" The shotgun cop leaned over the cubicle.

"I've got to hang up, buddy. Deep-dish pizza calls. I love you," Patrick said as he hurriedly replaced the receiver before Braden could respond.

And so now here he was, lying in this cell in his green robe and rouged cheeks with several other detainees, mostly drunks.

"Hey, freaky," said a voice from across the way.

Patrick opened his eyes to see a thin jackrabbit of a fellow standing at the bars of the cell opposite. He wore a black leather biker jacket punctuated all over with silver studs and racing pins.

"Yeah, you, freaky," the wiry biker said as he smiled. His sharp teeth looked as if they'd been purposely filed down to points. "You're the freakiest thing I've ever seen. In fact, you're freakier than freak. You're freakidiculous."

Patrick again closed his eyes, shutting out the sight of the black-leather lug-head.

"Did you hear what I said? That's freaky plus ridiculous."

Terrific, Patrick thought. Of all the bikers with whom to be incarcerated, he gets the one who's a budding linguist.

"Freakidiculous. That's what you are."

Patrick opened his eyes to offer an observation. "Is that the best you can do?" Patrick sat up, the day's disappointments having caught up to him, the fear for his son overtaking any sense of self-preservation. "Not 'curious,' 'odd,' 'idiosyncratic,' 'eccentric,' 'unorthodox,' or even 'weirdly peculiar'? Are you so stupid that you have to get two words wrong just to try and say one?"

"You better watch your mouth, man," the thin biker warned.

Patrick leaped up and grabbed his own bars and stared him down. "I better watch my mouth, man? How about 'Methinks you stinks, thou craven, addlepated foot-licker'?"

"You're talking some kind of trash. I'd shut my mouth if I was you."

"Scullion!" Patrick spit out.

Two more bikers grabbed the bars next to their friend. "What's going on, Breeze?"

Breeze pointed to Patrick and shook a greasy fingernail. "Green velvet dude called me an onion!"

Patrick laughed. He felt so full of fear he was fearless. "*Scullion*, thou clay-brained guts, thou knotty-pated fool."

"You don't be talking to Breeze like that."

"Silence, rampallian," Patrick hissed.

The third biker looked to the second. "You hear what he called you, High Ride?"

"Quiet yourself, fustilarian," Patrick turned on the third.

"You're a dead man!" yelled the third.

But Patrick just let it all out—the pain of standing accused of thievery by the very people whose affection he'd come to earn, the anguish of hearing Braden ask for a promised visit tomorrow, his dead wife's favorite dessert sitting on his son's tray and two spoons lying there instead of clinking together in her memory.

"You trunk of humours!" He gripped the bars and assailed the three bikers with the ancient insults. "You bolting hutch of beastliness, swollen parcel of drop-sies!" The three bikers stood dumbfounded as Patrick continued, "You huge bombard of sack! You stuffed cloak-bag of guts!"

"Shut up!" boomed out from behind the bikers.

"Shut up yourself, you . . . roasted Manningtree ox with pudding in his belly!"

The three bikers slowly looked behind them and then spread apart to reveal a cot in the cell's rear, from which a figure arose from its fraying mattress. It was a mountain of a man, clad in black leather like the rest, but unlike the rest, he wore a metal machine bolt dangling from each of his pierced ears like a fuel-injected Frankenstein.

"What'd you say to me, Meat?" the huge man said,

his voice hushed in a vapor of menace that made Patrick forget the protective steel bars and shrink back.

"I was not addressing you, good sir."

"He called you an ox that likes to eat pudding," the jackrabbit Breeze quickly said.

The huge Goliath biker stepped up to the bars himself and grabbed three with each hand. He kept silent for a small second, gathered his breath, and then bellowed a roar that thundered throughout the whole cell block. Inmates down the row began to shake their bars and shout. The place erupted into a chaos of howling mayhem as the two cops burst in, beating the cell bars with their batons, sending the inmates flying back into the rear of their cells.

"Knock it off, every one of you lowlifes! Who started this ruckus?"

The bikers pointed to Patrick. "He did!"

"All right, Jolly Green, let's go!" the driver cop shouted as he opened Patrick's cell and pulled him out.

"Am I getting out of here?" Patrick asked.

"You sure are," the shotgun cop answered. "You're headed to thirty-day lockup."

"What?"

"You've got no name."

"No address."

"No social."

"No one to post bail."

The two cops took turns reciting before they grabbed him by the arms. "You're headed to Riker's for a month-long wait to see the judge."

The policemen began to drag Patrick down the row of cells toward the open door leading into the main precinct.

And that's when it happened.

That's when Patrick Guthrie, drama teacher at Independence High School, father to Braden, widower of Linda, model citizen for almost all of his life . . . that's when he panicked.

The open door to the precinct was waiting.

Patrick threw off the two cops and bolted down the row of cells as the prisoners went wild with joy at the sight of the passing jailbird.

"Go, Freaky! Go!" Breeze cried.

"Run, Freaky! Run!" High Ride screamed.

And run Patrick did, through the door, down the outer hallway lined with mug-shot wanted posters, his green velvet robe flying out behind him.

"Prisoner in flight!" one of the cops yelled.

Police clerks and handcuffed perps alike were tossed out of Patrick's way as he made a mad dash through the detectives' room, past desks, around partitions, and finally nearing a door marked EXIT.

Patrick was almost to the door. *Almost free!* he shouted to himself in the midst of this unthinkable mania of escape. If he could just get through the door, he'd be fine. He would be by his son's hospital bedside before he knew it, like stepping through a mirror or falling down a rabbit hole. Once through the door he'd be home free.

Home.

Free.

He took the handle of the door and twisted it to suddenly find himself . . . locked in.

"We've got lockdown!" boomed a voice from behind him. "He's got nowhere to go, people!"

Patrick whirled around and spotted a stairwell. There was always somewhere to go.

Up the stairs he ran, taking the steps by two- and three-step bounds. Chasing footsteps echoed behind him like a thundering herd, but Patrick's raging panic forced him on, to what hope of escape he had no idea. But still he ran.

He'd seen the fruitless escapes on TV of jokers who'd got caught jacking some car and then led the police on an insane chase that only lengthened their jail time with each fugitive mile. And now here he was, leading the police on the same insane chase up the stairs and finally to a closed steel door at their top.

You're gonna get your keister kicked out there on the mean streets. Braden's voice echoed through his mind as he grabbed the steel door's handle, and it turned. Patrick was out in the night in a second. If only he could get to his son and spend a minute with him before he had to leave for prison, before Braden had to leave his world. He had to get off the roof.

But there was nowhere to go.

On all four sides of the roof, there was nothing but air. The city lights surrounded him in a swirl of multicolored stars, like a mock heaven that was beckoning him onward. Patrick looked back to see more than a dozen policemen pour out of the roof's door, guns drawn, and slowly come toward him.

"Get on the ground, hands folded behind your head, now!"

Patrick looked ahead of him. Nowhere to go but into the heaven of the colored lights and the air below that offered something that might just end up feeling like peace.

"Down on the ground! Don't make me say it again!"

Patrick walked ahead toward the far ledge and stood on the precipice and the promise of black oblivion far below. Could he do it? Why shouldn't he do it? He'd come to the end of all he could do for his son. Braden would be better off without him. He'd be better off with the man who hated Patrick and all he had done to take Linda away. Had he somehow helped to cause Linda's death? Had he somehow brought Braden to a place where his boy waited for an operation that might just cost him his life, and if it didn't, what kind of home did Patrick truly have to offer him?

Braden would be better off with another man as his father, a better man than he.

Patrick stood on the precipice, teetering on its edge, his green velvet robe flapping in the December night wind.

"Whatever you're thinking about doing, don't."

What *was* Patrick thinking about doing?

Leaving Braden behind to remember him as the man who left his son behind.

And that he would not do. There was a French vanilla dessert cup on a hospital tray waiting for him.
There were two spoons to clink. And whatever way it
was now bound to happen, there was a little boy who
was going to have his heart cut open and would have
to heal, and Patrick would never let him go through
that without his father.

Patrick turned back toward the approaching line of
policemen.

"Don't reach for anything! Hands behind the head!
It's over!"

Patrick dropped to his knees and put his hands
behind his head. "My name is Patrick Guthrie."

Yes. It was over.

Chapter 18

THE MAN WITH THE PLAN

etective Mike Kovach entered the interrogation room wearing a flannel sport coat that had seen better days and a wan face that had seen it all. He sat down at the plain wood table, ran his hand over the back of his neck, and looked to where Patrick sat behind the now peeled-off beard and wig. Patrick answered the detective's question before he had a chance to ask it.

"I did it to make enough money to pass a parental competency hearing. I did it so I wouldn't lose my son, for even a day. So you can drop me in a cellar and turn the lights out when you leave. I don't care."

Kovach nodded as opened a file and looked it over. "They tell me he's in St. Genevieve's."

"Until he has his heart procedure just before the holiday."

"That's what they also tell me," Kovach said as he leaned back in his chair. "Which is why I'm not going to slam you with resisting two law officers, attempted flight, disturbing the peace, and just plain stupidity above and beyond the highest heights."

Surprised, Patrick waited.

"I've got three daughters at home, and there's nothing I wouldn't do to see them every morn, noon, and night," he said as he closed the file. "I'm also glad you didn't take a header off my roof. That kind of *New York Post* front-page headline I don't need."

"So you're going to let me go?"

"I've got my informants, and with what they tell me I can put together a pretty good picture of what happened. You crossed some Christmas creeps and got good and framed."

"Is this going to go on my record?"

"You mean, will Family Court find out about this? No. You didn't hurt anybody and from what I understand from my boys in blue, you put on a pretty good show."

Patrick sat feeling relieved.

"But I'd stay off the street from now on. Next time something like this happens I'll be bound to make an official note of it, and I don't know a Family Court judge in the state who takes a shine to fathers who panhandle."

"What do I do now?" Patrick asked.

"What does your lawyer say?"

"I can't afford a lawyer."

"If you're fighting for custody of your kid, you're entitled to a free one from the state."

Patrick's face rose with hope.

Patrick stepped out of the 7th Precinct into the bitter December wind and wrapped the green velvet robe close around him as he headed down the sidewalk in search of a subway.

He would most likely lose his son, according to what the public defender had told him only a half-hour earlier. Maybe it would be for only a month or so until Patrick could get established in his new job, if that even came through in the New Year. But considering his circumstances and Ted's influence and wealth, any Family Court in the city would almost certainly rule that a child recovering from a heart operation would be better placed with the boy's grandfather.

And Patrick knew in his heart that it would be better for Braden, better for his healing body. But what would it do to the little boy's heart? Not the physical heart, which would certainly benefit from all that Ted could give him, but the emotional heart?

Ted hated Patrick. As he walked, he replayed the last memory he'd had of the old man throwing himself and Linda out into the cold that Christmas Eve two years before Braden was born. Patrick had agreed to go along with Linda and visit her father to explain in person that she was going to pursue a life in the theater. It was the hardest thing she'd ever had to do, but she did it, hoping with every fiber of her heart that her father would understand, might even wish her well.

But the old man had told them to leave. No matter that Patrick had a broken ankle, and there were no cabs to be had, and they had to walk across the Brooklyn Bridge at night just to get back to Manhattan. No matter that Linda was his only child.

It mattered like the devil to Linda, who saw all her overtures to her father ignored. And now it mattered like the devil to Patrick, who knew all Ted needed was a month with Braden to fill his mind with the idea that perhaps, just perhaps, his mother might not have died if she had had the regular physical checkups that an actor without health insurance could not afford.

It was this thought that Patrick could not brook. Once Ted was able to infiltrate the boy's mind with that idea, there might be no recovery.

Patrick turned the corner of Pitt Street and headed up Ninth Avenue. At this hour it was dark and empty. The city that never sleeps was out cold.

And then there they were.

There were six of them, shadows at first that emerged from below-street building stairwells. They approached Patrick in a slow wave, coming from both sides of the street across the pavement in an uneven parade. "And where do you think you're going?" one figure from the encroaching group asked.

Patrick said nothing.

"I'll tell you where you're going. The city morgue, that's where you're going," a second figure called out as he stepped into the glow of the streetlight. "You're gonna get yourself good and dead walking these bricks past beddie-bye."

It was Red-Beard and the back-alley boys. Patrick exhaled a relieved breath. "You guys? What are you doing here?"

"Checking up on you, making sure the cops know the score."

"You're the informants?"

"Undercover operatives," said Red-Beard. "Please. We do have our dignity."

"Of course. Well, in any case, thank you. You saved me."

"Not quite. You've still got a heck of a problem on your hands. No dad should lose his kid because of money, and not just before Christmas."

"Is there anything you don't know?"

"We know this," Red-Beard said as he held up a small white business card. "You should go pay a visit to a friend of ours."

Patrick stepped back. "I don't know."

"Go see him."

Red-Beard put the card into Patrick's hand and closed his fingers over the paper. "He's the man with the plan."

$C h a p t e r \quad 1 9$

SOMETHING'S CHANGED

The place used to be called Hell's Kitchen. It was one hundred square blocks of sooty brick buildings where gangs of Irish, Italians, and Puerto Ricans had rumbled for decades in back alleys. It was only a two-minute walk to the Actors' Studio and another minute past that to Broadway.

Back in the late 1990s, when Patrick and Linda were young actors, the rents had been low, so they'd moved into an apartment on the south side of 51st Street just west of Ninth Avenue. But now the neighborhood was called *Clinton*, and the sooty brick of the past had been power-washed and the windows underscored with flower boxes.

Patrick walked to his old stoop and looked up at the fire escape where he and Linda had spent so many evenings splitting a calzone and watching the street scene below. Shouting and boom boxes, hustlers and the odd grocer. Free entertainment.

But today it was all different. The abandoned building next door that had long been a nest for what you didn't want to know about was now a clothing boutique for kids. The local grocer was gone, and now that storefront was the face of a coffee chain. The corner of 51st and Tenth Avenue that Patrick passed had changed too. His blood was gone.

Nine Christmas Eves ago, Patrick was returning from a late rehearsal, and it was here on this corner that he had seen the first kid cross the street and then walk past him. But he hadn't seen the second, or the third. A minute later Patrick sat slumped against the cornerstone of a warehouse, wiping blood from his eyes.

Moments earlier, with the teenagers pounding away on him, he'd thought he was dead. The strange thing was that while the beating was happening, Patrick's mind had cleared a space apart from fear and pain and had the coherent thought that this was one heck of a lousy death scene. Only an actor would include in his final thoughts that he hadn't expected it to end quite like this, without even a deathbed speech. Patrick had to smile at the memory of his younger self.

There had only been this, his possible death coming at him from all angles for no discernible reason. And all he could think was *Death scene*. Then for no discernible reason life had its say as the kids abruptly ended the attack and moved on down the dark street, laughing at their handiwork with whoops and high-fives.

Patrick had risen to his feet and propped himself up against the building by putting both hands on the warehouse's side. He made his way back out onto the next avenue and tried in vain to hail a cab.

A half-hour later Linda had screamed as she looked up to see Patrick stumbling through the door, his face drenched in horror-movie red and reciting the words he had rehearsed his whole long way home: "It's not as bad as it looks. I promise. It really isn't."

And it really wasn't. His nose was broken, four of his ribs were cracked, but his pride was only bent. They waited longer for the nurse to bring the discharge papers than they had for the X-rays. So they spent the early morning hours of Christmas in the emergency room waiting to leave and making a vow to each other that this would be the only bad Christmas Eve they would ever have.

"But life doesn't make bargains." Patrick now stood on that same corner and looked at where his bloodstained handprints, which had actually soaked into the stone and stayed for several years, were now gone, power-washed away, no doubt. No trace left of that long-ago drama.

Now he had a new one, and just as much of a life-or-death one as that had been. He couldn't beg on the streets anymore, and the money he'd made in the last two weeks had only paid his bills and one month's rent. The bad Santa had robbed him of the chance to get ahead and show Rebecca and the court that he could take care of his own son. He could chance it and find another corner to work, another disguise, but any possibility of arrest and its appearing on his record for good was too great a risk. He could lose Braden forever.

So, walking through his completely new old neighborhood was the only choice left to him. Patrick checked the address on the card Red-Beard had given him last night and made his way up Ninth Avenue, tracking the numerically ascending addresses.

He wasn't even sure Red-Beard wasn't leading him into some kind of lion's pit. How well did he know this guy, really? He didn't. And in truth he didn't even know his or any of their real names. Patrick had been beaten up here once. You can change a neighborhood's name, but you can't change the world's danger. But still Patrick walked on. What choice did he have?

Boutique after boutique interrupted by the odd internet café led him up the avenue. He had told Braden he'd be pulling a double shift at the pizza place. Patrick had wanted to open the vanilla yogurts and have their spoon-clinking toast, but the boy shook his head.

"We'll do it tonight, Dad. After you take care of whatever it is you're so worried about."

"I'm worried about *you*," Patrick said before he could stop himself. He hadn't told Braden about Ted seeking custody. As far as the boy was concerned, Rebecca had been just a social worker checking up on Braden's welfare. Patrick and Rebecca had agreed beforehand that was all the boy needed to know.

"You've been worried about me since I was born, and especially these last two weeks. But now it's different, it's worse, and you're not hiding it very good."

"Very *well*," Patrick said.

"Correcting my words isn't going to make me think things are the same today as they were yesterday. Something's changed."

"Something's changed" echoed through Patrick's brain as he passed another internet café and then found himself standing in front of an unexpected sight.

It was a storefront that actually belonged to the twentieth century. It might have even belonged to the century before that by the looks of it, for it wasn't really a store but a bar, and it didn't have a front so much as it had a door with a sign that unceremoniously demanded that all customers "USE THE BACK WAY OR YOU'LL GET KICKED . . . NO IFS OR ANDS, JUST BUTTS."

"Lovely," Patrick declared as his eyes passed over the faded place. Its two windows wore Erin's harps painted in peeling gold. The antique bar stood on the sidewalk between the internet café to its right and a pet-grooming salon to its left, looking like a piece of

West Side history some development committee forgot to unpreserve.

To Patrick's eyes, it looked like a watering hole that must have been frequented back in the day by the Westies, the Irish mob who controlled Hell's Kitchen for decades until a series of arrests sent them to jail or scattered to the other boroughs.

But here this place still sat, now in Clinton, like an aging thug who refused to retire to Florida or take refuge in Paraguay. It had stood its ground and eyed with suspicion the shifting parade of yuppies, Generation-X'ers, urban bo-bo's, and post–9/11 metrosexuals. A gamey old grand-da perched on his porch year after year.

Spying the opening to a small alley on the bar's left side, Patrick squeezed through a thin, rusting gate and walked down the passageway through piles of beer crates and kegs. He finally reached what he took to be the back door, even though it stood on the building's left side, for there was no more of the alley beyond it, only a cinder-block wall with metal spikes rising from its stony ten-foot top.

Patrick grabbed the handle to the gray metal door and pulled it open.

Chapter 20

STRIFE, WIFE, OR LIFE

Patrick entered a dimly lit stockroom stuffed with liquor cases stacked on top of a row of old pinball machines. He closed the door behind him and walked under the lone hanging bulb, which flickered as if it had been sent from central casting for a camco in a splatter movie but then had stopped in here for a drink, never to leave.

Patrick worked his way to the far side of the room and entered an open hallway, better lit and filled with the sound of distant music. As he headed toward the light of the bar, the music grew louder—if you could call violins loud.

For that's what it was, classical music on high volume. As he drew nearer, Patrick recognized the piece. It wasn't "classical" in the technical sense of the word; it was Baroque. The last sound Patrick had expected to hear drifting down this hallway, lined with old photos of boxers and racehorses dead and gone, was the second movement of Arcangelo Corelli's *Christmas Concerto*.

Patrick entered the bar. In the left corner, on top of the sawdust-covered floorboards and under a host of old promotional beer mirrors, were two violins, a viola, and a wide cello. Patrick stood amazed and watched four young people, music students surely, work their strings into the movement's swelling finale.

Two dates flooded Patrick's mind: 1690, the year the piece was written, and 1999, the year the piece was performed at his and Linda's wedding by just such a string quartet as this. It was so unexpected, so incongruent in this rough-and-tumble tavern, that his heart rose with the music's crescendo, for it had to be a sign from Linda or God or someone that everything was going to be all right after all. The quartet brought the Baroque piece to its climactic forte and then finished with a final triumphant coda. Then silence.

Patrick burst into applause, clapping with unbound appreciation.

The musicians looked at him as if he were a lunatic.

Patrick kept applauding, and then he turned around to the rest of the room to see that not only was he the only one clapping, but every one of the ragtag rummies who sat spread out behind the tables and at the bar's counter were also all staring at him as if he'd lost his mind.

Patrick stopped clapping and took in the group of sneering red noses. "It's one of my favorite concertos."

Silence.

"Of all the concertos Corelli wrote, or even Bach or Vivaldi, that has to be my favorite."

Hard stares.

"That music was played when I married my wife, okay?" Patrick panned a defiant gaze across the room.

Nobody said a word or moved until one particularly large man rose from his bar stool and approached with an empty glass mug clutched in his hand. The empty mug was soon resting on Patrick's shoulder as the big rummy put his arm around his neck and leaned into his face, breathing, "That's a beautiful story. If you buy me a beer, I'll listen to it all over again."

The bar broke out into a storm of laughter.

"That's all right. I don't think it went over very well the first time," Patrick said as he moved away from him and toward the bar. Beyond it, tarps and paint cans lay on the floor before the blocked front door clearly under renovation.

"Come on!" cried the big rummy after the retreating Patrick. "You had me at Bach and Vivaldi."

More laughter from the tables as Patrick approached the bartender standing behind a great, scrolled wooden counter large enough to look as if it had been carved out of the hull of a clipper ship. The bartender's wide frame matched the wood he stood behind, and he looked away from Patrick down to an unscrewed tap handle he was polishing.

Patrick couldn't help himself. "Why is a string quartet playing in a sawdust saloon?"

"It keeps out the riffraff," the bartender said as he screwed the tap handle back.

Patrick looked at the patron sitting on a stool next to him, who grinned with all twelve of his teeth. "It does?" Patrick asked, looking back at the bartender, who finally raised his eyes.

"None of these fellas you see here carry heat."

"Excuse me?"

The bartender finished screwing the tap handle and impatiently wiped the bar where Patrick had rested his hands. "I don't care for firearms in my establishment, and I've never known a villain who could come in here with his guns and his drugs and sit more than ten minutes while that noise is playing. By the time the second string song is starting up, they're out the door looking for some other place to peddle their poison. Works every time."

"Well, I wouldn't call Corelli noise—"

"These fellas here can stand it. Sure, they start tipping a few come noontime, but they're good boys, all of them." The bartender stopped wiping the wood and studied Patrick. "Are you planning on being a good boy in here?"

The question took Patrick aback as he saw the bartender grip something unseen under the bar, then nodded in agreement. "I plan on being a very good boy in here."

The wide man smiled. "Happy to hear it."

Patrick pulled out the calling card. "I'm told I can find this man in your establishment."

The bartender took no more than a glance at the

card before looking down to where he resumed wiping. "What would you want with him?"

"I understand he's a lawyer. I've got a problem."

"Strife, wife, or life?"

"I don't understand," Patrick said.

The bartender stopped wiping and clutched two bottles in the well below his waist. "If you're looking to sit with the counselor, you'll need to ante up," he said, and nodded to the very far back corner. There sat a heavy, carved-oak booth where the back of an equally aged white-haired head appeared.

The bartender set down a glass on the bar. "A dram of scotch is what'll get you seated across from the counselor. But your problem will be selecting what label I pour."

The bartender reached down to the low-shelf well and lifted a scotch bottle with a bagpiper on the label. "Is it strife? You've got a moving violation on your record you'd like moved somewhere else? You've got a zoning issue you'd like reinterpreted for the city?"

The bartender took a bottle off the glass shelf directly behind him bearing a wax seal. "Is it wife? You've got an affair of the heart you'd like to straighten out? Maybe it's your affair. Maybe it's one belonging to your wife. Love has flown out the door and you don't want to be the one stuck with all its droppings."

Then the bartender nodded high up the bar where just under the ceiling hung a shelf lined with spirits looking as ancient as a pantheon of vintage deities. "Or is it life?" He looked Patrick straight in the face. "No explanation needed."

"It's life," Patrick said.

The bartender rolled a ladder down the length of the bar, climbed up its dozen or so steps, and fished down a dark flagon made not of glass or metal, but of stone. The wide man blew off a layer of dust that flew into the air like so many collected years now drifting down to settle on the floor.

Patrick watched the glass fill to the halfway mark.

"That'll be forty dollars."

Patrick's face fell. It was the price of a top-shelf drink in Monte Carlo, maybe. And this place wasn't Monte Carlo. But Patrick paid from the street money the cops had given back to him, then set down a generous tip. "Merry Christmas."

Patrick picked up the glass and turned to go, but

the bartender suddenly grabbed his arm without spilling the expensive liquor. At first Patrick thought he'd offended him, but the bartender simply raised the stone flagon again and topped off the glass.

"God's grace to your life."

Chapter 21

NEWMANS

From the looks of the man who glanced up at him from the wood booth, Patrick was going to need all of God's grace he could get.

The man's hair was as white and disheveled as a wintry trash heap. Both eyes were road-mapped with dead-end blood vessels. And the only thing redder than his cheeks was his nose, which had enough blue mixed into its bulbous flesh to flirt with purple.

The man addressed Patrick, "Do you stand before me with a purpose? Or have you picked this very spot to forever lead the life of a statue?"

"I have a purpose," Patrick answered.

"I would say your primary purpose is to set that glass before me. If you wish to pursue a second purpose, you may take a seat. But the latter is of small consequence to me compared to the former."

Patrick put the glass down in front of the ruddy fellow and took a seat in the booth across from him. "Mr. McManus, I've come to ask your—"

But Patrick was silenced by a raised left hand that slightly shook as Mr. McManus, keeping his right hand on the table, closed his eyes and lowered his lips to the glass, taking a large sip of the liquor. He let the alcohol travel through his veins to work a path into his raised palm, which now steadied before Patrick's eyes. McManus opened his eyes appreciatively. "I discern that your troubles are quite dire."

"They are. My son—"

Again, the hand was raised, albeit steadily this time. "*Usquebach*."

"What?"

"*Usquebach*," Mr. McManus said in a matter-of-fact manner as he acknowledged the glass. "It's an ancient Gaelic derivation of *uisque beatha,* meaning 'water of life.'"

"That's very interesting, Mr. McManus," said Patrick, who couldn't have found it less so.

"Call me Abe."

"Very well, Abe. My son is in St. Genevieve's Hospital—"

"Your son?"

"Yes, my son. If I might be able to simply tell you my problem, then—"

"How old is your son?"

"Eight."

"And he's sick?"

"Yes," Patrick replied with a growing impatience. "He's eight and he's ill, but he's going to have a procedure that will change all that. What I need is representation to handle a custody hearing in Family Court. His grandfather's trying to take him away from me."

"I can't help you, Mr. . . . whatever your name might be."

"But you haven't even heard my whole story!"

The bartender frowned and looked over at the booth.

"You haven't heard my story," Patrick said again in a whisper.

"No need to hear any more. You've got an ill child

under the age of eighteen. I don't take cases involving Newmans."

"Newmans? What's that supposed to mean in ancient Gaelic?" Patrick asked as his impatience began to fester into fury.

"It's my own word for new humans. 'Newmans.' Mr. . . . ?"

"Guthrie."

"Mr. Guthrie, I don't take cases involving children, at least living children. The unknowns are too numerous. The child's illness can always take an unexpected turn, perhaps morphing into something that changes the complexion of the case entirely, and then you have to begin the process all over again with a new jury and new appeals and re-appeals."

"But this is not a case about his illness. It's a fight to keep my son from being taken away from me," Patrick said and pounded his fist once on the table.

"Pipe down back there," the bartender barked.

"I can see that our conference is coming to an end," Abe McManus said as he went to lift the scotch glass, but Patrick grabbed it first. He threw the glass, and it smashed in the empty corner opposite the string quartet, which abruptly stopped playing.

"That'll be enough of that!" the bartender yelled as he hopped over his counter.

But Patrick wasn't aware of the wide man wading through all the patrons who'd risen to their feet in excitement. He pounded his fist on the booth again as Abe McManus could only stare at his precious "water of life" dripping down the near wall.

"Do you know how old that scotch was?"

Patrick was lifted from his seat by the bartender and hauled across the room as the patrons chanted in unison, "Eighty-sixed! Eighty-sixed! Eighty-sixed!"

Past the racehorses and boxers Patrick was roughly escorted by the bartender and a rummy. Past the dead pinball machines and liquor boxes and out into the alley, where he was tossed into metal trash cans, slamming into the brick wall behind them and landing facedown in a crate of empty peanut shells. Patrick rose to his feet, spitting out a shell and then a mouthful of blood.

"I see your face back here, boyo, you'll be coughing up your whole spleen." The bartender and the patron went back inside and slammed the metal door behind them.

Patrick staggered up the alley back to the street's sidewalk, where several people immediately shrunk away from the bleeding man.

It's not as bad as it looks. I promise. The words played in Patrick's head, anxious to be rehearsed and delivered to a beloved wife waiting at home, sure to be horrified, certain to comfort and heal.

But there was no one at home this December. And the last thing he'd do was bring this latest bruising into Braden's life.

A couple of Christmas shoppers pointed to his bloodied face and hurried away across the street. Maybe the old neighborhood hadn't changed that much after all.

Patrick stopped and looked at himself in the window of the pet-grooming salon. His lip was split, but not bad enough for stitches. Still, it would need to be explained to Braden somehow.

A golden retriever wearing a yuletide ribbon around its neck looked up from its crate and cocked its head at Patrick's dabbing at his mouth with his shirt. The two met eyes.

"It's not as bad as it looks," Patrick mouthed to the dog. "I promise."

Abe sat at the booth and recovered from the unexpected altercation, which had upset the pleasant and eventless Saturday morning he'd planned for himself.

"There you go, McManus," the bartender said as he set down another dram of the expensive scotch. "Seeing as how your drink ended up on the wall, this one's on the house."

"I appreciate a good pun, but that isn't one."

"What did that nutter want anyway?"

"Something about keeping his child."

Abe lifted the glass to his lip, but then caught sight of himself in a promotional beer mirror. He set the glass down, untouched.

The two vanilla yogurts sat on the hospital tray unopened next to two unused spoons.

The man standing in the room's open doorway thought the hour was late for dessert, especially as the boy lay sleeping, his thin neck and face propped with pillows toward a television playing a pirate ghost movie. Just behind it, the window showed a thick wintry downfall.

But instinctively the boy opened his eyes and saw the stranger standing in his doorway. "Who are you?" Braden asked, his voice barely above a whisper.

"Abe McManus. I know your father."

"Are you his friend?"

"Not precisely."

Abe felt a rough hand on the back of his neck.

"What do you think you're doing, talking to my son?" Patrick said as he pulled Abe out of the doorway and down the hall.

"Actually, I came to speak with you."

Patrick yanked Abe into a hallway bathroom, then closed and locked the door. "Any talking between us was over this afternoon when I found myself face-down and bleeding into a trash can."

"I am compelled to say, Mr. Guthrie, that misfortune was of your own making. You don't toss sixty-nine-year-old scotch or break a two-dollar glass. They're equal crimes at the Erin's Harp."

"What do you want?"

"To help you with your problem."

"I don't want your help. You don't know anything about my problem."

"I know you're facing a custody battle against a bitter father who's never gotten over his daughter's sudden death, and a powerful grandfather who's looking to take his grandson away from you, you who owe rent, can barely keep your bulbs alight, heat in your vents, or your phone connected. Normally a grandparent would not have a hope of obtaining custody from a biological parent, but your circumstances have not only leveled the playing field, but the boy's condition has wildly slanted it in his direction. Do I have a proper command of your problem?"

Patrick leaned back against the bathroom wall. "I'd say that sums it up beautifully."

Abe McManus sat down on the closed toilet seat and crossed his legs. "I'm going to help you fight this."

"Why the change of heart?"

"I could bore you with my regrets, or I could convince you I'm willing to represent a man brave enough to declare his love for Corelli in a bar full of barbarians. The truth lies somewhere in between."

After a pause, Abe shrugged. "I like you."

"Fair enough. But if you're to help me, no drinking on the job, right?"

"As of this moment, I'm on the wagon."

The two shook hands.

By the time Abe McManus had left the hospital, Patrick was again by his son's bedside. One spoon was in his hand and the other spoon was in Braden's. "Here's to Mom's favorite yogurt and a merry Christmas."

They clinked spoons and dug in.

"Something's changed again," Braden said with a smile before taking a bite.

"Yes," Patrick replied, matching the boy's smile. "Something's changed again."

Chapter 22

LOVE DISAPPOINTED

A hand reached out and gently gripped Rebecca's shoulder. She opened her eyes to see a nurse standing before her.

"You can go up now, miss. Visiting hours began twenty minutes ago."

Two elevators and five corridors later, Rebecca stood in the doorway of Braden's hospital room, where the boy put a silencing finger to his lips and nodded at Patrick, snoring softly in the corner chair.

"I promise he doesn't usually snore," Braden whispered.

"Why should I care if he snores?" Rebecca softly asked, thrown by the boy's statement.

"When did you get here?"

"A few minutes ago."

Braden turned on the TV with the sound muted so as to not wake Patrick. "They've got all kinds of great channels on this set," the boy said, "including one that shows the lobby. I like to watch people come and go, sometimes even at four in the morning."

"All right," Rebecca conceded in more whispers. "I got here early. I was thinking about you."

"You're not just some social worker doing a regular checkup on a kid, are you?"

"Well, you're not just a regular kid."

"Something else is going on," Braden said, lifting his head.

Rebecca sat down and folded her hands. "Everyone wants what's best for you."

"What's best for me is snoring over there in that corner."

"Your father's a good man. He's done the best he can."

Braden propped up his body on thin arms and looked Rebecca straight in the face with the honesty that can only be offered by the very young. "He's done better than the best he can, because he's done it without telling me everything that's going on."

Braden pointed to his father.

"This is the person who'd do anything for me, just like he did for Mom. Did you know he dressed up as a blender one Christmas and turned himself into Sir Christmas Mix so he could pay the lighting bill? And he'd do it again to pay for the lights."

Rebecca's face flooded with a realization. "Or the heating bill or the rent," she said as she sat back with the truth taking hold of her.

"Of course he would."

Rebecca looked to the sleeping man.

"He might even wear a green robe and a beard with a wreath around his head and call himself the Ghost of Christmas Present."

The orderlies wheeled Braden down the hallway as Dr. Friedman looked back at Patrick. "We'll be down in Imaging." Then she looked at Braden on the gurney. "Last MRI, okay, champ?"

"Okay. I don't mind the tight tunnel. No needles there."

Patrick watched his son being rolled away and then turned back to Rebecca. "What did you want to talk about? I really should be with him."

"Where were you last night?"

The question took Patrick aback. "Where I am every night, the deep-dish—"

"No. You've been fired. Wally said he couldn't take your being late anymore. I guess you'll find out when you go there tonight."

Patrick sat down and ran his hand across his face. "I've got money, and I've got another job lined up for the New Year, a copywriter position at an advertising firm."

"Can anyone there substantiate that?"

"Not until the New Year. Why can't this Family Court hearing wait until then?"

"Because your son's operation happens before then," Rebecca said, and then she pulled out another official-looking notice. "And the hearing's been moved up yet again. In light of your new unemployed circumstances, the case has been expedited through the court system."

"You mean Ted Cake's been spying on me, knows I've lost this last job, and is pushing you around like a red wagon."

"I resent that."

Patrick stood. "I resent that my son will be placed in the hands of a man who's just dying for a chance to convince him that I'm somehow responsible for the loss of his mother."

"You don't know that."

"Don't I? When I called Ted after he didn't come to his own daughter's funeral, he blamed me. He held me accountable for not being able to take care of her."

"Then call him again. Maybe you can remedy this."

Patrick paced the hallway tile. "I won't talk to that bitter and deluded old man. I won't make that mistake again."

"What's without remedy should be without regard."

Patrick stopped. "What?"

"Isn't that what you said to me out on Broadway that one day?" Rebecca looked him full in the face. "The Ghost of Christmas Present?"

Patrick sat back down in silence.

"Whatever happened between you and your father-in-law has a remedy. All hate has a remedy, because hate is only love disappointed. Call your father-in-law. That's the remedy."

Patrick looked at her. "How long have you known?"

"Since about a half-hour ago, Sir Christmas Mix." Rebecca smiled.

Patrick looked down the hall after Braden, who was just being wheeled onto an elevator, then back to Rebecca.

"The hearing is two days from now," she said as she put the notice in Patrick's hand.

"But Braden's procedure is tomorrow morning."

"Which is why they're not holding it until the day after tomorrow. Now that you're out of work, Ted Cake's really putting the pressure on."

"What are you going to tell them?"

Rebecca ran a gentle hand over Patrick's jagged hairline.

"The truth."

Chapter 23

THE SECOND SUNDAY

It was the second Sunday of December, and Patrick was giving thanks.

Tomorrow morning Braden would have his heart operation. His arteries were large enough to sustain the procedure, his last MRI showed all other organs in good working order, and all food had been restricted until Braden woke from the anesthesia and could be thoroughly examined. So here they sat again, father and son, with a lone ginger ale between them on the hospital tray.

"Want some more soda?" Patrick asked.

"You're learning, Pop. Soon you're gonna be a real New Yorker."

"And soon you're gonna be out of here and back in school."

"And back home with you, right?"

Patrick looked away out the window and reached for his son's hand. "I wanted to talk about that when you were through with the operation and recovering. There might be a better place for you to go and heal, buddy."

"It's Mom's dad, isn't it?"

Patrick looked at Braden, who tried to pull himself up.

"I'm going home with you."

"He's got everything I can't give you, like light and heat."

"But you've made enough on the streets to cover that."

"He can arrange a private nurse, take you on vacations, give you—" Patrick stopped mid-sentence and just stared at the boy. "What did you say?"

Braden lay back and smiled. "You've made enough on the streets as the Ghost of Christmas Present."

"How did you figure that out from a hospital bed?"

"I watched Ms. Brody figure it out. She's the one who's going to decide where I go, right?"

"She's just going to testify. A court's going to decide the day after tomorrow, while you're here recovering."

"What is she going to tell them?"

"She said the truth."

"Maybe the judge will be a Dickens fan."

"That's what I'll do, put on my green velvet robe wearing a beard and wig with a wreath around my head and plead my case."

"A wreath around your head? You're joking, right? You didn't! Oh, man, I wish I coulda seen that!"

"They loved me, I'm telling you."

Braden became serious. "Dad. No matter what happens, I know you did everything you could for me."

Patrick nodded. "I always will."

"But there's one more thing I want you to do for me."

Two hospital orderlies finished lifting Braden from his bed to the gurney and wrapping him in tight with a blanket. Dr. Friedman looked down at the boy. "Are you ready, champ?"

Braden looked to the far side of the room. "Are you ready, Dad?"

And there Patrick stood in his green velvet robe, beard, and wig, two Christmas ornaments dangling from his ears and a wreath around his head. "As ready as I'll ever be," he said.

"Nerves? Don't worry. If you can play Broadway and 34th, you can play these hallways."

Patrick took his place at the head of the gurney and then led it out of the room as the orderlies rolled it into the hallway and down past patients' rooms. They proceeded for a couple of steps until Braden finally nudged his father with his bare foot. "Come on, Dad."

Patrick cleared his throat as they passed nurses, doctors, patients, and families, who all stared at the passing vision of the Ghost of Christmas Present. "God rest ye merry gentlemen, let nothing you dismay."

His song carried and echoed down the tiled hallway like a host of deep-voiced elves calling ahead to all who gathered. They came from sick rooms and hallways, staff desks and utility closets, to stand in doorways to watch Patrick and Braden pass by.

"Remember Christ our Savior was born on Christmas Day."

Braden grinned at the people they rolled past. "That's my dad."

Medical staff, patients, and families all began to clap and join in singing the haunting, familiar old carol. "To save us all from Satan's power when we had gone astray."

And as the man in the green velvet robe and wreathed head walked on, they sang, "Oh tidings of comfort and joy, comfort and joy," their voices filling the hospital hallways.

"That's my dad."

Chapter 24

HOLIDAY HOBGOBLIN

Christmas shoppers spilled out of stores and flowed into waterways of pedestrians streaming down the sidewalks of lower Midtown Manhattan. On Lafayette Street, storefront windows displayed small forests of carefully placed poinsettias.

If there were any storybook church bells ringing, you couldn't hear them for the honking of taxi horns and an exchange between two cabbies that didn't quite dovetail with the spirit of the holiday. Epithets were tossed back and forth across the two lanes of traffic, as were several hand gestures that transcend the divides of culture and language.

The Ghost of Christmas Present was not here with Ebenezer Scrooge at his side to sprinkle his magic, glitter dust on the two cabbies, and cause them to merrily shake hands and then go off arm in arm in search of a Christmas goose and plum pudding. The Ghost of Christmas Present was standing in a courthouse hallway nearby, wearing a jacket and tie, having just finished telling Abe McManus the truth.

"Boyo, oh boyo," Abe said as he took an uneasy seat in a wooden chair along the wall.

"I thought you should know how I've made my money this month."

"Thank you for telling me. I wished I'd known earlier. You would have saved me a journey into my conscience. That's what I get for looking at myself in a beer mirror."

"You wouldn't have taken my case."

"I would have offered pro bono to the other side."

"I did what I had to do to keep my son."

"By dressing up as a holiday hobgoblin?" Abe said, his voice carrying through the halls of justice.

"I was the Ghost of Christmas Present, the very first embodiment of Father Christmas—"

"Save it. Just tell me, who else knows about this?"

"She does," Patrick said, nodding to Rebecca, who entered the courthouse hallway clutching her briefcase and walked past them without a nod.

"The caseworker?" Abe said as he shook his head. "Does she have any film of you? Any eyewitnesses who can identify you as this Ghost of Christmas Present?"

"None that I know of."

Abe's mood rose. But then Patrick's dipped. "Unless she's talked with any of the staff, patients, or patients' relatives who were in the hallway of St. Genevieve's Hospital yesterday morning."

"You didn't."

"My son asked that I walk him to the operating room as the Ghost."

"You know you've undone yourself?"

Patrick sat with the truth of it. "Maybe I meant to. Who am I to keep my son all to myself in an apartment where I don't know if I'll be able to pay the rent or utilities?"

"You said you had a new job."

"But how long will that last, the way the world's turning these days? Until Easter? The Fourth of July? Then what do I do? Hit the streets as Peter Rabbit or Uncle Sam? Forget it."

Patrick rose and straightened out his jacket and tie. "If my boy ends up hating me after what Ted tells him, so be it. I'd rather have Braden turn his heart against me for allowing his mother to die than for his heart to turn against his own body because he wasn't getting the right care. I've been selfish to think otherwise." Patrick looked down the hallway at an approaching group of people. "He'll be safe with Ted Cake."

And indeed, it was Ted Cake who approached with Mila and a couple of lawyers in tow. The two met eyes for a second, and then more than a second as neither one would blink and look away from the other.

"Good morrow, good sir," Patrick said as Ted was just about to pass by. The older man hesitated for a second, looking back at his former son-in-law for a bewildered second, but then briskly walked on into the courtroom followed by Mila and the lawyers.

"What was that?" Abe said.

"Just a greeting from an old friend. If the truth's going to come out, it might as well come out now."

"Listen to me. Silence your tongue now if you're hoping for any kind of visitation. If they truly can confirm that you've been prancing around the streets in a velvet robe and wreath around your head for money, the only time you'll spend with Braden is once a month under the eyes of a court-ordered supervisor. Do you understand?"

Patrick nodded.

"Now let me do the talking and, for the love of Braden, keep the Ghost of Christmas Present inside the book and outside this court."

Abe headed into the Family Courtroom followed by his client.

Chapter 25

A NUTCRACKER READY
FOR HIS NEXT WALNUT

Patrick sat in the defendant's chair and fingered his Captain Pluton Band-Aid.

Mila watched him do it.

"All rise. Hear ye, hear ye, the Family Court for the District of Manhattan is now in session. The Honorable Judge Donald Ramirez presiding."

Patrick rose and looked at Ted, who kept his face fixed straight ahead and his hands folded down like stiff marble limbs that might crack off at any second from strain. Yep, the old man still hated his guts. *No matter*, Patrick thought. *The boy is all*.

"All having business before this honorable court

draw near, give attention, and you shall be heard. You may be seated."

Patrick and all sat back down as Judge Ramirez, middle-aged but with an already full head of white hair, looked over the court papers. "In the case of Theodore Cake, the plaintiff, versus Patrick Guthrie, the defendant, is counsel ready to proceed with opening statements?"

Ted's lawyer rose like a nutcracker ready for his next walnut. "We are, Your Honor. We intend to prove that the defendant, Patrick Guthrie, is unfit to care for his ten-year-old son, Braden, who is, while I speak, recovering from an invasive heart procedure. Mr. Guthrie was terminated from his teaching job the Friday after Thanksgiving, could only obtain temporary employment at a pizza restaurant, and was terminated from that job this past Saturday for continually being late and then finally not showing up for work at all."

Judge Ramirez glanced at Patrick with a dim face.

"Furthermore, Mr. Guthrie is behind on his rent, light, heat, and phone bills. He is mere weeks from being evicted. This is not only an unfit environment for a child, it is an unthinkable one for a child recovering from heart surgery. We ask that Braden Guthrie be placed in the care of Mr. Cake, the father of the boy's mother who tragically passed away some three years ago. We ask that Mr. Cake be awarded indefinite custody of his grandchild. It may be that Mr. Guthrie could very well obtain employment in the New Year, but his recent work history shows that he is unstable and even incapable of preserving the most modest of jobs. Put frankly, the man can't even show up to cut a pizza, let alone care for another human being."

The Nutcracker sat down and Ted looked over at Patrick with satisfaction.

"Is opposing counsel ready to make an opening statement?"

Abe wasn't. He just sat there as if he were the cracked nut and the Dance of the Sugar plum Fairy had just scattered the broken bits of his shell all over the courtroom.

"Mr. MacManus?"

Abe looked at Patrick, who whispered, "Just tell the truth."

"And end up begging out on the streets with you?

I'm too old to play Punxsutawney Phil come February . . . or maybe I'm not." Abe rose and collected himself. "I will tell this court the truth."

"Seeing as how you're a member of the New York Bar, I hope so," Ramirez said with a voice as dry as gravel.

"Patrick Guthrie has done everything he can to take care of his son. Throughout this holiday season he has embodied the very spirit of Christmas. Even though he has faced his son's impending operation with a father's natural fears, he has spoken and sung his way through his days and into the hearts of those around him."

Mila smiled to herself and again looked at Patrick, who still fingered the Band-Aid. Rebecca sat several rows behind, clutching her file.

"He has brought yuletide joy to many who needed it most." Abe sat down as the bewildered judge looked from Abe to the opposing counsel and then back again.

"Mr. McManus. That's your opening statement?"

Abe put his head in his hands and nodded. Ramirez shrugged and looked back to the plaintiff's table. "Call your first witness."

*R*ebecca stood at the witness box as the bailiff swore her in. "... and nothing but the truth, so help you God."

"I do." Rebecca sat as Ted's attorney approached.

"Ms. Brody. You have interviewed Mr. Guthrie and observed his living and working situation now for some two weeks. Is that correct?"

"Yes."

"And have you come to a conclusion as to whether Mr. Guthrie is a fit parent to take care of a young boy who's recovering from very serious heart surgery?"

Rebecca sat silent for a moment, her eyes traveling from Ted to Patrick and then back to Ted, who began to glower. "Mr. Guthrie is the best father to that boy any man could be."

The attorney traded disappointed glances with Ted. "That's not what I asked, Ms. Brody. Is Mr. Guthrie a fit father to care for a fragile child? Is he financially capable? Are his living situation and home life ones that you would consider acceptable?"

"Mr. Guthrie assures me that he will have gainful employment come the New Year. I believe him. Until that happens, there are financial aid programs to explore, city assistance—"

"Ms. Brody—"

"The boy shouldn't be without his father," Rebecca said in rush of words.

The attorney again looked to Ted Cake, who gave a knowing nod. "Ms. Brody, isn't it true that in observing and interviewing Mr. Guthrie, you have gone above and beyond what a city social worker would be expected to do?"

"I've done my job."

"Does your job include staying with Mr. Guthrie and his son for a whole showing of an animated movie at the hospital?"

Rebecca tried to answer, but was cut off.

"Does your job include arriving at the hospital at four in the morning in preparation to see the father and son?"

Rebecca looked to Ted and realized she'd been followed.

"Isn't it true that you've become emotionally attached to this man?"

"I wouldn't say that."

The attorney picked up a paper from the plaintiff's

table. "Just like you became emotionally attached to a fellow colleague during your medical internship, Julia Bright, and forged her signature on a patient's chart?"

"So she could sleep. She hadn't had any sleep for two days and was bumping into carts while making decisions."

"So you took it upon yourself to forge her signature on a chart, just as you took it upon yourself not to disclose the AMA censure to the city when you applied to be a social worker, just as you're now taking it upon yourself to decide that Mr. Guthrie is fit to take care of his child even though he can't pay for his rent, light, heat . . . Do I have to go on?"

Rebecca sat in the witness box, exposed and beaten up. "Yes."

"Yes what?"

"Yes," Rebecca said as she looked straight at Patrick. "I'm taking it upon myself to tell you that Patrick Guthrie would do anything, and I mean anything, for his son. And if it please the court, I perjured myself earlier."

Ramirez sat up as Rebecca kept her eyes on Patrick.

"Go ahead and hold me in contempt. I'm very emotionally attached to Mr. Guthrie."

Chapter 26

WHERE PLAYACTING ENDS
AND REAL LIFE BEGINS

Ted Cake sat on the witness stand in his custom-cut suit and silk tie like victory itself, beautifully gift-wrapped and waiting to be opened upon the judge's eventual decision—which would certainly now go his way once this needless proceeding was over.

"So in your opinion, Mr. Cake," his own attorney said as he crossed the floor toward Patrick, "Mr. Guthrie here is entirely incapable of caring for a child, let alone one who suffers from a life-threatening condition."

"In my opinion, sir, Mr. Guthrie is not capable of taking care of anyone or anything, and clearly that includes himself."

Abe rose. "Objection, Your Honor. The issue at hand is the welfare of the son, not the father."

"We would argue those two issues go hand in hand," said Ted's attorney.

"The court would agree. Objection overruled."

Abe, deflated, sat back in his chair as Patrick leaned over to him. "This isn't going our way."

"I need a drink."

"You need to call me to the stand."

Ramirez banged his gavel at the audible whispering. Abe and Patrick quieted.

"So, Mr. Cake," Ted's attorney said, walking back toward the witness box. "What makes you so certain of Mr. Guthrie's ineptitude at caring for his boy?"

Ted looked straight at Patrick with a stare brimming with what Rebecca now recognized as love disappointed . . . hatred.

"I am certain Mr. Guthrie is inept at caring for the boy because he was completely inept at caring for the boy's mother. She died for lack of regular physical examinations."

Patrick bolted up. "Linda's heart condition was asymptomatic," he said, regurgitating word-for-word the explanations every doctor had offered. "Only three percent of people who have an enlarged heart are ever even diagnosed."

"Sit down and silence yourself, Mr. Guthrie!" Ramirez said.

Ted continued. "She would have been part of that three percent if she'd had proper medical insurance and care, if she'd had the proper sense to stay away from a layabout thespian who couldn't tell you the difference between where playacting ends and real life begins."

Abe sprang to his feet again. "Now this truly is conjecture and character assassination!"

Ramirez brought his gavel down again. "The court has no choice but to sustain the objection." Ramirez turned an eye to Ted. "Mr. Cake, please confine your answers to the questions posed."

"May it please the court," the attorney said, "Mr. Cake's concerns are for the welfare of his grandson and it is clearly his opinion Mr. Guthrie's life in the theater is a direct obstacle to that welfare. May we pose a direct question to our client along those lines?"

Ramirez nodded. "You may."

"Mr. Cake, is it your opinion that your ex–son-in-law's former profession as an actor not only directly led to the lack of medical care for your daughter—"

"Objection!"

"I'll allow it."

"—but also led to his being let go as a teacher with no seniority, and finally fired from a waiter position that even the most amateur of actors can maintain?"

Ted once again stared at Patrick, who willed himself not to look away.

"It is my opinion that Mr. Guthrie's acting life has caused only loss and death. He prefers to pretend rather than face his real responsibilities as a husband and father. Nothing good has come from it, certainly not to my life."

This last statement washed over Patrick's face, and his eyes filled with thought. He gripped the table with hands desperate to feel their way through a hard decision—whether to protect the small part of life left to him or risk it all for the large part of life he just might win.

"The plaintiff rests," Ted's attorney said and sat down.

Patrick's eyes wandered across the room for an answer to the question that was pounding through his mind and heart. He turned the Band-Aid round and round his finger as his eyes landed on Mila, sitting behind the plaintiff's table. She was looking straight at Captain Pluton before lifting her gaze up to Patrick.

"Hello, Ghost," she mouthed in a whisper.

Patrick saw it. His face flooded with decision as he leaned over close to Abe's ear and whispered something urgent. Abe tried to shake Patrick off for a second, but finally relented as Ted stood up to leave the witness box.

"Mr. Cake? The defense has a question of its own."

Ted reluctantly sat back down. "I would think this court has all the answers it needs."

"You'll answer all appropriate questions, sir," Ramirez said.

"Of course, so long as they are just that." Ted watched contemptuously as what he viewed as a two-bit lawyer rose and approached him.

"Mr. Cake, you stated just now that Mr. Guthrie's passion for the theater has caused you and your loved ones only heartache."

"That's correct. In my opinion, my daughter would be here today if it weren't for that."

"So as you've said, nothing good has come of it, certainly not in your life."

Ted's attorney rose. "Objection. This line of questioning is leading nowhere."

"You began this line of questioning, counsel. Sit down," Ramirez said.

Abe continued as he paced across the floor, "So you've never attended any of Mr. Guthrie's performances?"

"Certainly not."

"And if you did so, you would find nothing good in them—no comfort, no laughter, no joy, no self-reflection, no balm of the soul?"

Patrick shot a look to Abe to get on with it.

"In other words, as certain as you are that Mr. Guthrie's love of the theater took your daughter from you, you are just as certain that you have never been touched by it."

"Of course not. I don't have to put my hand on a Bible to swear to that."

Abe turned and looked to the defendant's table. "Then the defense calls Patrick Guthrie to the stand."

Chapter 27

TO THINE OWN SELF

Abe leaned into Patrick and whispered as low as he could. "Are you certain you want to do this thing?"

"Into the breach," Patrick said back just as softly.

"Mr. MacManus," Ramirez said as he leaned toward both of them. "Mr. Guthrie is in the witness box so that we all might hear what he has to say. Being a member of the New York Bar, you probably are already aware of that."

"Yes, Your Honor." Abe drew back from Patrick and collected himself. "Mr. Guthrie, what is your profession?"

"My first calling was to the life of the theater."

Ted rolled his eyes.

"My second calling was teaching drama to high school students."

"And are you gainfully employed in either of those professions at the moment?"

"No."

"Are you gainfully employed in any profession at the moment?"

"I was fired from my waiter position, though I do have a verbal promise of employment as a copywriter at an advertising firm come the New Year."

"But that is not official yet?"

"It is not official."

"So I ask again, are you gainfully employed at the moment?"

"No," Patrick said as he looked at Ted, who nodded with satisfaction. Ramirez sat back.

"So you have made little to no money at all this Christmas season?"

Patrick hesitated for a second, catching Rebecca's eyes. "I have made close to three thousand dollars," he said.

Ramirez sat up, along with Ted and the Nutcracker attorney.

"And how did you accomplish that?"

Patrick hesitated again, knowing his next answer would expose him as not only a beggar, but a man "unstable" enough to take to the streets dressed in the green velvet costume of a fictional Christmas character to perform for coin . . .

In other words, a nut job.

"I'll ask again," Abe said, giving the suddenly silent Patrick a glower. "And how did you accomplish that?"

"I begged for money."

The courtroom held only a dozen people, between the judge, bailiff, attorneys, and witnesses. But the gasp that went up was worthy of a packed house.

"You what?" Ramirez said, his face dropping in disbelief. Even Ted was too surprised to be pleased.

"I begged for money. I stood on the sidewalk of Broadway and 34th Street and asked people for cash, currency . . . coin of the realm. I became a panhandler."

Ted's eyes narrowed slightly as he mouthed to himself, "Broadway and 34th?"

"And how did you panhandle—just as you are now?"

"No. I wore a costume, a Christmas costume. People love a good character, and I gave them one of the best Charles Dickens ever wrote."

Ted's face ripened with a growing realization as he turned and looked back at Mila, who smiled.

"What was this character you speak of?"

"I was the Ghost of Christmas Present, the original embodiment of Father Christmas. I was a singing, rhyming, Shakespeare-reciting spirit who haunted the sidewalks of Broadway"—Patrick looked straight at Ted—"and gave maybe just a little joy to those who approached me."

Ted bolted up. "It's impossible! I would have known you."

"Mr. Cake! Sit down!" Ramirez said, banging his gavel. Ted sat down, looking wildly unbalanced.

Patrick met his eyes. "Spare some coin for a poor beggar, sir," he said in his Ghost voice. "It'll secure you a place in heaven."

Ted gripped the plaintiff's table and steadied himself.

"So it would seem that Mr. Cake's declaration that he has never seen nor been affected by one of your performances might now be in question."

The Nutcracker attorney bolted up. "This line of questioning is absurd. Whether Mr. Cake did or did not know this man was a begging Ghost of Christmas Past—"

"Present," Abe said.

"Immaterial! That Mr. Cake perhaps stopped to hear a pathetic wretch on the sidewalk and toss him a nickel—"

"It grew to be ten dollars a day," Patrick said.

"Immaterial!"

"Once he even gave me a hundred-dollar bill."

"So, he's a man generous to unfortunates. No one disputes that. But that he was an unknowing audience to the man he knows to be an unfit provider for his grandson changes nothing."

"It was your own client who declared he blamed the defendant's pursuit of acting for his daughter's death, and that he has also never been touched by it, so much so that he would put his hand to a Bible to that effect. Ten dollars a day to a panhandler tells me he just might have been touched."

"So my client was 'touched,'" the Nutcracker said in exasperation. "But that doesn't make Mr. Cake a redeemed Scrooge ready to buy everybody in town a fat goose, and it doesn't make his grandson Tiny Tim. That's a Christmas fairy tale and this is real life. Braden Guthrie's welfare is what's at stake here."

Patrick lowered his head, and Ted's attorney took note of it.

"The plaintiff moves that the court make a decision now based on the defendant's own admission that he is not only unemployed, but financially desperate enough to dress up in a Christmas pageant costume and publicly beg for money."

Ramirez nodded to himself and thought hard under a silence that hung in the courtroom like a ripening storm cloud.

Patrick sat in the witness box and looked to Ted. "I did it for Braden."

"The witness will silence himself," Ramirez said.

Still, Patrick looked at Ted. "I loved her, too."

"I'll say it one more time. The witness will silence himself."

"Every Christmas she'd wait for you to arrive at our door. Every New Year's, Easter, Fourth of July."

"You are dangerously close to being held in contempt, Mr. Guthrie."

Yet Patrick continued to address Ted, both men

locking eyes. "Every performance, she'd search the audience for the sight of you, a man she always knew had been secretly denied the opportunity to be an actor himself, and now looked to deny her the same thing."

"Mr. Guthrie!" Ramirez said as he slammed his gavel down. "Not one more word, sir. I warn you."

Patrick sat in the witness box; all was lost except maybe the truth. "To thine own self be true," he said to Ted, who finally looked away.

"Bailiff," Ramirez said, "arrest Mr. Guthrie for contempt of court."

The bailiff approached Patrick and lifted him by the arm to his feet. Ted did not watch as Patrick was cuffed and led out of the witness box and toward the prisoner's exit. Patrick was to the door and almost out of the court when Ted turned back.

"And it follows, the day the night," Ted said.

Ramirez held up his hand for the bailiff to stop.

"Thou cannot then be false to any man."

"What is this?" Ramirez could only ask.

"*Hamlet*," Patrick and Ted said in unison.

"I know it's Shakespeare. They don't let you be a judge unless you've attended high school. I mean, what is *this?*" Ramirez looked at both Abe and the Nutcracker attorney. "What's going on between plaintiff and defendant?"

"This man isn't the defendant," Ted said. "He's my son-in-law." Ted looked at Patrick, tears filling his eyes. "I miss her so."

Chapter 28

THE THIRD THURSDAY

It was the third Thursday of November, and Ted Cake was giving thanks.

Today there was turkey, cranberry sauce on the side, stuffing moist enough to not have to worry about strategically hiding it under a drumstick so as to not offend the chef, and a mince pie that Mila had sent from London.

And today there was also Braden at his left, Rebecca at his right, and Patrick at the table's other end.

"You have a quote for every occasion, Patrick. Please say grace." Ted watched Patrick trade surprised glances with Braden and Rebecca, then nervously bow his head.

The old man smiled to himself and bowed his head as well.

Patrick hesitated, and then began. "I have lifted up mine eyes unto the hills. From whence cometh help? My help cometh even from the Lord which hath made heaven and earth."

Ted raised his head and thought for a second. "Shakespeare sonnet?"

Patrick gave Ted a wide grin. "The Book of Common Prayer."

Braden chuckled. "Dad knew you'd put him on the spot, Grandpa. So he remembered the Lord helps those who help themselves."

The whole table erupted into laughter as the plates began to be passed around, and the room began to fill not only with Thanksgiving, but with the spirit of many Christmases yet to come.

Acknowledgments

This book would not be in its present form without the generous support of Becky Nesbitt, the incisive and thoughtful editing of Holly Halverson, and the cheerful assistance of Jessica Wong.

Thanks also go to Wendy Heller, Esq., for her legal services and advice.

And finally, the kindness and encouragement of our literary manager, Carey Nelson Burch, has been invaluable.

Printed in the United States
By Bookmasters